THE HOUSE OF THE PELICAN

By the same author
THE REIVER'S ROAD

THE HOUSE OF THE PELICAN

ELISABETH KYLE

ILLUSTRATED BY PEGGY FORTNUM

THOMAS NELSON AND SONS LTD
LONDON EDINBURGH PARIS MELBOURNE
TORONTO AND NEW YORK

THOMAS NELSON AND SONS LTD
Parkside Works Edinburgh 9
36 Park Street London W1
312 Flinders Street Melbourne C1
218 Grand Parade Centre   Cape Town

THOMAS NELSON AND SONS (CANADA) LTD
91–93 Wellington Street West   Toronto 1

THOMAS NELSON AND SONS
19 East 47th Street New York 17

SOCIÉTÉ FRANÇAISE D'EDITIONS NELSON
25 rue Henri Barbusse Paris V^e

First published 1954

CONTENTS

I	Rooms to Let	1
II	Railway Encounters	8
III	Effie and the Blue Fish	20
IV	Dungeons and Jewels	30
V	A Sea-Lion in the House	41
VI	The Outlook Tower	57
VII	Teaching Janet a Lesson	70
VIII	The House of the Pelican	80
IX	The Mystery of Mr and Mrs Bond	90
X	On the Trail	101
XI	The Little Gold Box	109
XII	A Cat and a Clue	119
XIII	Dead-End	129
XIV	Maisie Paterson	138
XV	The Disappearance of Effie	151
XVI	Through the Fence	161
XVII	Effie says 'No'	175
XVIII	Pins	182
XIX	John Jamieson's Fish Supper	194
XX	Mr Bloomfield makes a Deal	205
XXI	John Jamieson seeks a New Home	212
XXII	It's an Ill Wind . . .	220
XXIII	The Farewell Symphony	231
XXIV	A Letter from America	239

LIST OF ILLUSTRATIONS

'I wanted to see where she was going'	*Frontispiece*
There really were no more chocolates	11
There stood the strange woman	25
Maybe he shouldn't have come	31
They were sitting farther along the seat	47
They were playing a queer old game	65
Leaning over the sill and laughing	147
A separate little dwelling	163
They should not have been allowed on the scene	223

Chapter I

ROOMS TO LET

'EXCUSE me—this *is* Caroline Square?'

The man who asked the question looked rather thin, rather shabby, and very anxious about something. He was carrying a queer oblong case in one hand, but the Edinburgh citizen whom he had stopped didn't bother to take time to consider what was in it. He was in a hurry himself.

'Ay,' he said, and broke into a run because he heard his tramcar in the distance, passing the end of the Square.

The man with the queer-looking case had wanted to ask something else, but he wasn't given time. Instead, he stood where he was, peering about him to see which was

THE HOUSE OF THE PELICAN

Number Seven. The Square consisted of grey houses ranged round an untidy garden. Everything looked a little decayed, but that was to the good, because then the boarding-house he was looking for couldn't be dear. All the same, knowing the favour he was about to ask, he still felt nervous. At the moment the Square seemed empty and deserted. He began to walk round it, screwing his eyes up short-sightedly, reading the numbers.

Farther along a girl came out of one of the houses and began polishing a big brass plate on the door. She looked about fourteen or fifteen, and was wearing a bright-green sweater and a grey tweed skirt. The man was very quick at guessing what other people were thinking. He knew somehow that the girl was nervous, nervous of having people see her polish the brass plate. Every now and then she would give a glance over her shoulder to make sure no-one was coming. When she did that, the large glossy horse-tail of fair hair, tied right above the nape of her neck with green ribbon, jumped up.

But he had to speak to her all the same. When he drew level with the steps he saw that the house *was* Number Seven; and that the brass plate said MRS MACKENDRICK, BOARD RESIDENCE. He cleared his throat and ran up the steps till he stood beside her.

'Pardon me,' he said, 'but could I have a word with Mrs MacKendrick?'

The girl noticed at once that he spoke with an English accent. Also, she took time to wonder what was in the queer-looking case. 'I'm afraid you can't,' she said. 'Mother's gone out.'

'Oh.' He looked disappointed. 'Are you Miss MacKendrick?'

She felt pleased, because any girl is pleased at being treated as a grown-up when she is barely fifteen. 'I'm Chris MacKendrick. Is it—is it about rooms?' And she looked at the queerly shaped case again.

'Yes, it is. I'm a member of the New English Orchestra, which is giving a series of concerts during the Festival. Unfortunately I didn't book rooms before coming up here, and now every place seems full. But one of the tourist offices gave this address——'

'You're playing at the Festival?' she broke in eagerly.

Chris was not a good-looking girl by any means. She had rather a puddingy face and knew it. But it lit up and looked quite attractive when she was interested and thrilled about anything. She was obviously thrilled now.

'I always hoped some real musicians and artists would come here! But the big ones all go to the grand hotels on Princes Street, and Mother won't have theatre people because she thinks they'd come in late——'

'Don't mistake me,' the man interrupted hastily. 'I'm only an ordinary trombone player. I don't even play solo. And—I want accommodation for my family as well.'

'Where are they, and how many?'

'Just a son and daughter, and they're arriving from London tonight. My name's Foley, and my boy's called Pat. He's about your age. He'd be no trouble at all. My wife's dead, unfortunately. Pat and I could share a room, and if you had a little one for Janet . . .'

He held his breath as he mentioned Janet. He hoped she would ask no questions. It was because of Janet that he had been trudging about all morning, trying to find

THE HOUSE OF THE PELICAN

some place to stay in. ('No children,' everyone said. And, 'I'm sorry, your little girl is too young. . . .')

But Chris was so pleased at the thought of letting those two empty rooms, she forgot to ask how old Janet was. One person had written cancelling her room, and the other had stayed one night and then said the bed was too uncomfortable to sleep on. The beds *were* uncomfortable, but that was because new mattresses were so expensive to buy. And charwomen were expensive too, which was why Chris had to help her mother in the holidays by sweeping the steps and polishing the big brass plate.

'Come in and I'll show you the rooms,' she said hurriedly, adding, because she liked the look of Mr Foley, 'I'm sorry you saw me polishing the plate, but it couldn't be helped.'

' "Who sweeps a room as for Thy laws," ' Mr Foley quoted, stepping into the hall, ' " makes that, and th'action fine." '

'What?' Chris shut the door. 'Oh, poetry. Of course I'm not so silly as to mind doing house-work. But people might think we hadn't enough service and they wouldn't be comfortable. So they wouldn't take our rooms.'

'Don't you worry about that,' Mr Foley assured her hastily. 'I'm certainly taking the rooms.'

The house was a big one and very shabby. Mrs MacKendrick had been left it by an uncle, and as she was a widow with very little money to live on, she had turned it into a boarding-house. The trouble was, she never had enough money to get it freshly done up, so the people who came here did not pay her very much. Only during

Edinburgh's yearly Festival of Music and the Arts was she sure of letting all her rooms at once. And even now, there were those two at the top of the house, left empty just when everyone had booked their accommodation elsewhere. . . .

'Very nice, very nice indeed,' Mr Foley was saying absently as he looked around the big attic with the two iron bedsteads and all the marks on the faded wallpaper. 'This will do excellently for Pat and me.'

Chris was sorry for him. Men could be taken in as easy as winking, her mother always said, specially when they hadn't got wives to look after them. She felt suddenly that she *must* be honest about the mattresses.

'They're rather hard,' she said, patting the nearest. 'I—I don't want you to do without sleep, so that you can't play your trombone properly.'

'Pat and I can sleep on anything so long as it's flat,' Mr Foley assured her, adding, after a glance, 'or even fairly flat.'

They went into the room next door, a much smaller one, almost a cupboard, with a sloping roof and a small skylight window let into it. Strangely enough, Mr Foley looked quite approvingly at the window.

'Nobody could possibly fall out of that,' he said.

Chris looked astonished. Again Mr Foley recognised a danger signal. In another minute she would ask Janet's age. 'I think I left my trombone in the other room,' he said hastily; 'would you like to see it?'

So they went back and took the trombone out of its case. Chris had never seen one close to before, and she thought it a very odd shape. Mr Foley put the mouthpiece to his lips and blew a long melancholy sound. He showed her how, by sliding a bar along with his free hand, he could increase the column of air he was blowing down the tube, so as to cover more notes. He said there were four trombone players in his orchestra, and that sometimes the first trombone player had a little solo to play all by himself. Otherwise they all played together, and nobody in an audience could distinguish Mr Foley's playing from the rest.

'I'm just a cog in a wheel,' he said, sighing a little, 'just a useful cog.'

Chris felt sorry for him again. 'I'd give a lot to be a solo player myself,' she confided, ' but I can't play anything, so what's the use ? '

It was true ; she sometimes imagined what it would be like to wear a beautiful long dress off the shoulders and have her face all painted up so that nobody saw the freckles, and stand on the edge of the Usher Hall playing the violin—or the cello or harp. Though you had to sit down to the cello, and harps were always at the back, she noticed. Each year during the Festival the newspapers were full of pictures of this or that world-wide artist. Chris envied them greatly but, being a sensible girl, had not allowed herself to dream of anything more than the possible arrival of some glamorous artist to stay at the guest-house.

And now a trombone player *had* come. He wasn't very glamorous, but he was better than nothing. At least he was one of the Festival performers, even though he didn't play solo. And he had a girl called Janet, which would be nice in a houseful of grown-ups. Perhaps she and Janet could go to some of the Festival things together. . . .

Mr Foley was thinking of Janet too. They had reached the front door again, when he said abruptly, ' About Janet. Pat's quite an independent boy, he can look after himself. But I'll be out nearly all day at rehearsals, and then, of course, the concerts at night. Would you—would you mind just keeping an eye on her ? '

' I'll take her around,' Chris promised largely ; adding, ' we do have some help for an hour or two every day. And it's my holiday too. I don't see why Janet and I shouldn't go around together a bit.'

A curious look passed over the new boarder's face. But he only said goodbye and began going down the steps again. Chris had almost shut the door when she heard him reascending them in a great hurry.

' I almost forgot ! ' he was saying. ' Pat and Janet arrive at six-thirty tonight, and I can't possibly meet the London train, as the concert begins at seven. You—you couldn't meet them instead, and bring them here, could you ? '

Chris looked doubtful. ' I could meet the train all right, but it's always crowded. And I don't know what they look like, so how can I find them ? '

He avoided describing them, saying, ' Oh, that's all right. They'll be waiting beside the ticket collector, and Pat's going to carry a copy of *The Musical World*. He's about your age and height, you know, so you can't mistake him. And he'll have Janet beside him, of course.'

Before Chris could ask what Janet looked like he had run down the steps again, and was making his way, with a load off his mind, towards the nearest tram stop and the beflagged gaiety of Edinburgh's more fashionable centre.

Chapter II

RAILWAY ENCOUNTERS

The London express was more crowded than usual. Even the first-class carriages were full, and Willington Peabody Bloomfield was glad to leave his parents now and then and prop himself up in the corridor instead.

The Bloomfields were Americans, and they were bound for the Edinburgh Festival. Mrs Bloomfield had belonged to Boston before her marriage, so she was very fond of culture. Mr Bloomfield was even more cultured than his wife, because he played the piano rather well, though just as an amateur, of course, and, being very rich, was one of the chief guarantors of the Fairport Symphony Orchestra, Fairport, Mass.

Their son Willington was not cultured at all, and had no intention of being so if he could help it. He viewed this excursion to Edinburgh with deep suspicion, rightly guessing that it would be used to instruct him in history and the arts. He was glad when he encountered, in the corridor, another boy of about his own age who was also going to Edinburgh. He seemed a very decent sort of fellow with no English swank about him. Willington (called Will for short) hoped they might come across each other later, and said so.

Pat Foley looked pleased, but shook his head regretfully. 'You're travelling first-class, aren't you? That means you'll be staying at one of the big hotels. Father's gone on ahead as usual, and he'll have taken rooms in some measly part of the town. We can't generally afford anything else.'

'That sounds as if you moved about a good bit,' Will suggested.

'Oh, didn't I tell you? My father plays in an orchestra, so he has to. In term time I'm at school of course, and our landlady looks after my kid sister. But the old man likes to have us tooling along with him during the holidays.'

'You don't play anything yourself, do you?' Will eyed his new friend with alarm and suspicion.

'Got no ear at all, I'm afraid. It's a great grief to the old man, but it can't be helped. Janet—my sister, you know—will probably end up on the stage. She plays like mad to the gallery already.'

Janet, sitting wedged in the third-class carriage from which her brother had escaped, began to feel restless. She was just nine years old, and a remarkably pretty child. The Foleys' kind old London landlady delighted in dressing her up to bring out the dark violet colour of her eyes, and secretly bought more expensive frocks and coats for her than Mr Foley could afford, paying the difference herself. Even after a long train journey, Janet still managed to look exquisite and uncrumpled. She loved clothes, and had insisted upon wearing her very best dress, so as to impress the other travellers on the train. . . .

Now she slipped off her seat and wandered out into the corridor, seeking amusement. The family filling up the rest of the Foleys' compartment had been very dull and had paid no attention to her at all. She drifted past several compartments until the occupant of one of them riveted her attention. A most beautiful lady sat in one corner, quite alone. Although it was still August, and warm, she had a luxurious fur cape round her shoulders, which Janet guessed would be delicious to stroke. Also, she had a large box of chocolates on her knee. She looked, too, as if she would have some lovely scent about her, so that the carriage would smell nice. Janet pushed the sliding door open gently. It *did* smell nice inside.

Madame Thérèse Martigny, of the *Comédie-Française*, looked up and smiled. She was coming to Edinburgh to give her world-famous performance of *Phèdre* and (while detesting air travel, so that she had chosen to come by train) was equally bored by the interminable journey to Scotland. What an exquisite child! She might furnish a little distraction. . . .

'*Viens, chérie!*' she exclaimed, patting the seat beside her and giving her famous smile. '*Comme tu es mignonne! Un bon-bon veux-tu?*'

She opened the box, and they were both disappointed

There really were no more chocolates

to find only one chocolate left. Janet was even more disappointed that the lady was foreign and so could not be talked to. Nobody knew better than Janet that a pretty dress is not enough, and that one has to have some conversation as well, in order to impress. Perhaps Madame Martigny felt a little the same. It was as if both actresses had forgotten their lines, and were therefore in danger of losing their audience. At any rate, after Janet had stroked the beautiful silver cape and satisfied herself that there were really no more chocolates, she gave her shy smile and left the compartment again. She had chosen her timing well, not staying an instant too long, in case the good impression made by her appearance should merge into boredom at her continued dumb presence. Subconsciously Madame Martigny recognised the fact, being skilled in exits herself. At any rate, she took the trouble to crane her neck, looking after the little figure as it wandered farther along the corridor and then disappeared into another compartment farther down.

It was the Bloomfields' compartment. The racks were filled with expensive luggage, but the scent here was just plain lavender water. Mrs Bloomfield used nothing else, and no make-up except a light dusting of face powder. She was wearing a neat tweed suit and a tight little old-fashioned turban with a game-cock's feather in it because she was going to Scotland. Mr Bloomfield looked incredibly clean and well shaved. He was a very tall man, and his legs stretched right across the floor.

Janet stepped over them daintily, smiling at Mrs Bloomfield.

'Why, dearie, where did *you* come from?' Mrs Bloomfield asked at once, in a very affectionate way.

'I grew lonely,' said Janet a little sadly; 'it's very lonely travelling alone.'

'Good gracious! You don't mean you're coming all the way up to Scotland by yourself!' Mrs Bloomfield gave a shocked look across at her husband, who gave a longer one over his newspaper at Janet. Mr Bloomfield was much cleverer at knowing people than his wife was. He had to be, as he was a business man.

'I've got a brother somewhere along the train, but he can't be bothered with me much,' Janet said more sadly still, 'and my mother's dead.'

'Poor child! What are you coming up to Scotland for then?'

'Because of the Festival. Father's there now. There was a band on the platform to meet him because he's so famous.' Janet climbed on to the seat beside Mrs Bloomfield and looked around under her eyelashes to see if there were any chocolates, but there weren't. So she went on talking about her father.

'When he's playing at concerts he wears white down the front and a white tie, and his coat's got long tails. And the people all cheer him like anything.'

Mr Bloomfield laid down his newspaper. 'What's your father's name?'

Janet wanted to make up a grand one, but there wasn't time. So she just said 'Lawson Foley' as importantly as she could.

'Lawson Foley? I don't seem to recollect—is he a singer or what?'

'He's a solo instrument—instrumentalist.' It was a phrase she had heard often, so she brought it out now.

'What's his instrument?'

'He plays the violin. He stands right out in front, all by himself, and plays it *beautifully*.'

Mr Bloomfield looked more puzzled than ever. He had heard all the world-famous violinists in his time, and he still did not recognise the name. 'I'm afraid I don't recollect——'

Just then, to her great relief, Janet caught sight of Pat wandering anxiously down the corridor in search of her. She knocked on the corridor window, forgetting that he was sure to give her away, and he stopped at once. There was a very tall boy behind him, who opened the door saying, 'Hullo, Pop, can I bring in Pat Foley? We've been getting acquainted. He's going to Edinburgh too.'

'Yes, of course, dear, but don't say " Pop ". I told you that before.' Mrs Bloomfield spoke for her husband, all in one breath.

Mr Bloomfield took a quick look at Pat, and liked what he saw. There was no nonsense about this fellow anyway. 'Come in, come in,' he said heartily ; 'we've just been getting to know your sister. She tells me your father is one of the artists appearing at the Festival.'

'He plays trombone with the New English Orchestra,' Pat said loudly and firmly to Janet's chagrin. The Bloomfields glanced across at each other over her head.

'But he *does* wear a white tie and a coat with long tails,' Janet protested.

'What hotel are you staying in?' Mr Bloomfield asked hastily.

'Oh, Father's probably taken digs somewhere. They're cheaper than a hotel. He can't meet us of course—he'll be at the concert hall. But I'm to hold this paper out in my hand, and he'll send someone to fetch us to wherever it is. He couldn't wire me before we started because he only got to Edinburgh this morning, and was going to search around.'

It all sounded rather haphazard to the Bloomfields, who had booked their entire trip, with accommodation, before leaving the States. Just then the train began to slow down. Quite suddenly they were in the heart of Edinburgh.

Everyone drew a deep breath. Mrs Bloomfield spoke first. 'Just think of the Castle!' she said reverently. 'Pure history in stone. We must read up about it, Willington. Remind me.'

'All right,' said Willington rather dejectedly.

But Pat craned his neck trying to see the Castle. 'I rather like drawbridges and things,' he said, 'and, with luck, there ought to be dungeons. Think of all that rock underneath it.'

'So there ought,' said Will, cheering up slightly. Dungeons would certainly be something.

Mr Bloomfield was a kindly man. He wanted his son to enjoy himself, and he didn't want him to be frozen off culture by too much history. 'You two might explore the Castle together,' he suggested. 'How would that do, Pat? Tell you what. As soon as you know where you are located, you might call Will up at the North Caledonian Hotel. Then we can plan some little outing for you both.'

Pat felt very pleased. He liked the Bloomfields, and only hoped Janet hadn't been making a little fool of herself before he came in. Perhaps she had, because they hadn't suggested her coming along too, which was a mercy. Just then, however, the train began running into the station, and he had only time to say hurriedly that he would most certainly telephone Will, when they had to go back to their own third-class compartment to collect the luggage.

The beautiful lady in the silver fox cape was leaving the train too. Janet stood, riveted, watching an elderly man, representing the Festival Committee, approach and hand her a bouquet. In her mind it was she who received the bouquet, and she intended to practise the gracious smile and the bow which Madame Martigny gave. Pat had to jerk her on quite roughly, towards the ticket barrier where a knot of people clustered to meet their friends.

Among them he saw a girl with her hands thrust into the pockets of her tweed coat and her hair done up with green ribbon. He was carrying his copy of *The Musical World* very prominently, and her eyes fell on it. The next moment she had stepped forward and was speaking to him.

'Are you Pat Foley? I'm Chris MacKendrick, and you're staying at our guest house. Where's your sister?'

'Here.' Janet had been hanging behind, trying to catch another glimpse of the beautiful Frenchwoman, and for the moment Chris hadn't noticed her. But Pat jerked her forward, and Chris tried not to look dismayed when she saw such a very little girl.

'I'll try and find you a taxi,' she said abruptly (thinking, 'I wonder what Mother will say!').

Janet sat still and did not speak at all in the taxi. She was suddenly dreadfully tired, and did not want to play the pretend-game any longer. Pat and Chris made a few shy remarks, and both were relieved when the taxi, after leaving behind it Princes Street with its gay crowds and decorations, ran down a steep hill towards a rather poorer part of the town, and stopped at Number Seven Caroline Square.

Mrs MacKendrick was in the hall. She had stopped on her way to the dining-room with a pile of supper dishes, because she had heard the taxi arrive outside. Once she had been fair, too, like Chris, but her hair was just sandy now, and though she was neatly dressed and looked brisk, there was always a look of worry on her face. The worry deepened when she caught sight of Janet, but the child looked so tired and white she had not the heart to be angry.

Instead, she handed the tray to Chris to finish setting the table, and took both the Foleys up to their rooms. She put Janet to bed at once, and said she would bring up her supper to her, though in the ordinary way she did not give trays in rooms because of the extra work. Then she went back to the dining-room again.

'I'm surprised at you, Chris!' she said reproachfully.

'I'm sorry, but I didn't know Janet was as young as that. I didn't really.'

Mrs MacKendrick's feelings swung round. 'Poor wee thing! Fancy her father dragging her round to strange places like this!'

'Well,' Chris pointed out reasonably, 'he couldn't do anything else, could he? Not if he was to see his children at all.'

'The boy seems a nice sensible lad,' Mrs MacKendrick began laying forks and knives down the table, 'but he'll just have to take charge of her most of the time. And you'll have to lend a hand too, Chris.'

The girl's heart sank. She remembered her promise

to Mr Foley, and realised now what it might entail. In the mornings she was supposed to help her mother to make the visitors' beds and so on, but in the afternoons she was free. Already she had been planning what she and Pat might do in the afternoons. But what fun would they have with Janet tagging along?

Chapter III

EFFIE AND THE BLUE FISH

PAT telephoned Will Bloomfield just after breakfast next morning, and they arranged to visit the Castle together.

'Father and Mother can't come—they're going to some exhibition or other,' Will told him; 'but Mother's given me the guide, and I've got to swot up a bit of the Castle history, just to keep her quiet. Still, I dare say we'll have a good time.'

Pat laid down the receiver, looking thoughtful. What about Janet? He went to find Chris, who was doing the landing with the electric sweeper. When she saw that he wanted to speak to her, she obediently switched it off.

'Do you like concerts?' he asked abruptly.

'I like the big ones in the Usher Hall. Why?'

'Because I'll ask father for two tickets, and you can take your mother to one, if you'll take charge of Janet this morning. Why don't you let her help you about the house? If you pinned an apron on her, she could quite easily play at being a housemaid or something.'

Chris nodded, feeling sorry for Pat, who immediately went out to meet Will Bloomfield. Meanwhile she found rather a pretty little apron and tied it round Janet, who was delighted. She gave the little girl a duster and took her into the drawing-room, a huge deserted-looking place full of heavy old-fashioned furniture, which felt cold even on this sunny day.

'How would you like to dust round here?' she said.

Fortunately Janet seemed quite pleased at the novel game. Chris watched for a moment, and saw that she was really very careful, and that she lifted every ornament gently before dusting under it. So she left her to herself and presently, in the bustle of the morning's work, forgot about her entirely.

Janet tiptoed quietly about the room for a little while, examining this and that, and dusting the legs of everything very carefully in between. Presently, however, she grew tired of playing at housemaid. She caught a glimpse of herself in the huge gilt-framed mirror which filled up nearly one wall, and did not like her apron any longer. Tearing it off, she took a bunch of rather withered flowers from the vase on top of the piano and advanced towards the mirror, holding the flowers like a bouquet.

'*Meevoo eskwissmee sarapandy*,' she said slowly and distinctly with a gracious smile. She tried to make it sound like the noises the beautiful lady had made at the station. She was the beautiful lady now—she could feel

THE HOUSE OF THE PELICAN

the soft furs at the back of her neck. And there, opposite her, framed in the mirror, was a little girl sent to give her a bouquet because she was so pretty and famous. The little girl smiled at her, held out the flowers. She put out her own hand to take them, and with the touch of the cold glass, the station, the crowds, the excitement going on behind her, all vanished away. . . .

She turned round, and there was the empty room. It seemed to become larger and emptier every minute, till she caught her breath with the cold of it. Father and Pat seemed far away, as in a dream. Everything here was strange as in a dream, and not nearly so real as the ones which came out of her mind. The big white door Chris had so firmly closed frightened her too. She dared not open it for fear of what might lie behind. . . .

She gave a little gulp and ran towards the window. Here the sight of the trees in the gardens and of a van driving round the Square reassured her. Something else, too, interested her and made her forget the cold feeling down her back. She was watching a fishwife come slowly towards Number Seven, carrying a large basket on her back by means of a leather strap which passed round her forehead.

The basket seemed heavy, by the way the woman

EFFIE AND THE BLUE FISH

leaned forward, straining against the strap. Janet wondered what it could possibly hold. She stuck her head out of the window to watch the woman, who halted suddenly, just in front of the house, and then disappeared down the area steps, giving a funny low call.

No longer frightened of the door, Janet rushed towards it and ran downstairs as hard as she could. She knew there was a basement under the ground floor somewhere, and that Mrs MacKendrick had brought up the breakfast things from down below. She pushed open the green-baize door, went down a rather dark flight of steps, and immediately felt the air blowing along the passage to meet her from the back door of the area.

There stood the strange woman, very square and bumpy about the waist, where her dull blue skirts were covered by a huge black apron slightly sprinkled with fish scales. When she saw Janet she called out, 'Good morning, ma lassie! It's Effie the Fishwife, and I've brought some fine fresh haddies for Mistress MacKendrick. Will I just come ben the kitchen and gut them for her?'

Janet didn't know what 'ben the kitchen' meant, but Effie soon showed her. Easing off the leather strap from her brow, she dumped the big basket on the step, opened it and took out some shining fish. Carrying them in her apron she marched down the passage and into the kitchen as if she knew the way well. Into her apron she had put, too, a sharp knife and a small wooden board like a bread board. She went over to the sink and began to gut the fish, slicing off their heads and tails and slitting them open with one deft stroke as they lay on her clean scrubbed board. Then she slapped the fish down on a plate, cleaned the board and the knife under the tap, and began to look round the room.

'Mistress MacKendrick aye leaves the fish money oot for me, if she's no' here,' she explained. Her eye caught a little pile of silver lying on the dresser. She went over to it, counted it, laid down some change in its place, and stuffed the silver into a capacious pocket under her apron.

Janet followed her down the passage to the area door, which Chris had left open in case Effie should come while she was upstairs doing the beds. 'What's in that big basket?' she asked curiously.

'Fish,' answered Effie, wasting no words. She heaved the basket on to her shoulders again, adjusting the strap round her head where it exactly fitted the red mark it had made across her forehead already.

Janet followed her out into the street and along the pavement, because Effie with her strange dress and speech fascinated her. Effie let her trot along by her side because she was well accustomed to being followed by children, and she did not realise that Janet, being a stranger, might not be able to find her way back to Caroline Square.

'Where do you live, Effie?' Janet asked.

'Awa' doon at Leith, where the fishing-boats come in.

There stood the strange woman

I've a nice wee hoose wi' a red roof and twa china dogs on my mantelpiece. Ye'll need to come and tak' tea wi' me there some time.'

Janet's eyes sparkled. 'Thanks, I'd love to!' she said.

They had turned out of the Square now, and were on a steep road with tram lines running down the middle. A tram stopped just opposite, and who should step out of it but Mr Foley, carrying his trombone in its case, just returning from the morning's rehearsal. Janet said goodbye hurriedly to Effie and ran to meet her father, who seemed astonished to see her.

'Where's Pat?' he said, looking around.

'Oh, he went out after breakfast to meet that boy on the train. Did you have a good rehearsal this morning? Was Mr Buxbaum angry or nice?'

Mr Buxbaum was the conductor of the New English Orchestra. Sometimes he was nice, but if anything went wrong he was apt to fly into awful rages. When that happened, and particularly if the trombones were at fault, Mr Foley would come home quite upset. He was upset now, but not because of Mr Buxbaum.

'I told you you were never to go out alone,' he said very severely.

'I wasn't alone. I was with Effie.'

'Who's Effie?'

'She's awfully nice. She wears a leather strap round her head, and a big basket, and three or four petticoats that bunch her out——'

'Don't talk nonsense. Look, there's Mrs MacKendrick coming along. You don't want Mrs MacKendrick to know you're a naughty girl and make up stories?'

They were nearly home now, and there was Mrs

THE HOUSE OF THE PELICAN

MacKendrick coming towards the house too, from the other end of the Square. Mr Foley lifted his hat politely. Mrs MacKendrick had been shopping and carried a good many parcels. She smiled at them both, and said, 'Hullo, Janet, have you been meeting your father?'

'She slipped out alone, I'm sorry to say,' Mr Foley said.

'I *wasn't* alone!' Janet said indignantly. 'I was with Effie, and she's going to ask me to tea. She's got a little house all made of glass with a red roof. And inside it, she's got a pet lion and two dogs, but the dogs are made of china——'

Mr Foley stopped half-way up the steps. 'Listen, Janet, I've told you you're too old now to make up stories. It's all very well when you're grown-up and can write them down and sell them. But if you tell them to people, and expect them to believe you——'

'But I *did* go with Effie!' Janet was almost crying now. 'And she wears queer bunchy skirts, and keeps a great big fish in her basket. It's all blue—I saw it—with teeth. She cut off a piece for Mrs MacKendrick. . . .'

Mrs MacKendrick was fitting her latch-key into the door. As it swung open she turned back, laughing. 'That's Effie all right, Mr Foley. She's the fishwife who calls here every Thursday. But I doubt it wasn't a blue fish she had in her basket; it would just be plain haddocks.'

Janet fled through the door and disappeared up the staircase. Mr Foley paused in the hall. He looked rather miserable and worried.

'That's it, Mrs MacKendrick. Part of Janet's story was all right, but she made up the rest. All that nonsense about Effie living in a glass house with china dogs. When she was little, she made up fantastic stories; I suppose all children do. Now she's beginning to mix them with fact, and really, it's very difficult——'

'I dare say Effie would have china dogs all right. They made them at the potteries in Portobello long ago, and nearly all fishwives have a pair. Don't you bother, Mr Foley. The child will grow out of it.'

'But I *am* bothering!' Mr Foley burst out. 'I don't like the way she makes up things at the drop of a hat. I don't like a child of mine to tell lies. Pat never did. Perhaps I haven't been strict enough with her, but it's really very difficult for a man to bring up a child of nine. If only her mother had been alive!'

Mrs MacKendrick looked sympathetic. Poor Mr Foley sounded quite desperate. Such a nice quiet man too, and having to trail his children about like that! 'Never you mind,' she told him; 'I'll speak to Janet next time she tells a tarradiddle. It's certainly time she learned the difference between fact and fiction.'

Chapter IV

DUNGEONS AND JEWELS

A LITTLE while before this, Pat Foley had entered the foyer of the North Caledonian Hotel and was looking shyly about him. Compared with the quiet shabby boarding-house he had come from, this place was a palace. The cream-and-gold decorations were imposing, and the crowds of smart people eddying about confused him, making him aware of his shabby old suit.

He wished he had had the sense to put on his best one. Everyone here was *so* well-dressed, and there were a lot of foreigners too ; not foreigners like old Buxbaum with his baggy suit and drooping moustache, but tall Scandinavians and glossy-looking Latins—no doubt they would be famous solo artists—and quite a good sprinkling of Americans.

Americans undertook so much, they were apt to forget some arrangements they'd made. Perhaps Will Bloomfield had forgotten about this one. No doubt he had gone out already with his parents, in the big touring car he had said his father was sure to hire, if they didn't actually buy one. Pat began to feel hot under the gaze of the nearest hotel porter. Maybe he shouldn't have come. . . .

And then he saw the Bloomfields stepping out of the lift, all three of them. They looked quite pleased to see him too. In fact, Mr and Mrs Bloomfield were delighted that Willington had found what Mr Bloomfield called a nice straight fellow to go around with. He and his wife

Maybe he shouldn't have come

were going to a morning concert, so they parted just outside the hotel.

There was no difficulty about finding the way to the Castle. There it was, towering on its crag to the left of them. The two boys began walking up the steep hill towards it, and presently found themselves in a narrow street called the Royal Mile because it ran for that distance between the Castle at one end and the ancient Palace of Holyroodhouse at the other.

'Gee! Look at the height of those houses, and all crushed up together like that!' They weren't anything like the skyscrapers at home, of course, but Will looked at them respectfully none the less. High, narrow, with crow-stepped gables, they had been squeezed together on the rock, centuries ago, so as to be under the protection of the Castle's guns. Once they had been the town houses of the nobles about the court of Mary Queen of Scots, and many still bore weathered coats-of-arms above their doorways leading to the courtyards within.

Now they were slums. Poor people passed in and out of the doorways under the chipped coronets of stone and the queer heraldic animals which sometimes supported them. There were a good many public houses, and even more antique shops because of the tourists who explored the Royal Mile in droves every summer. But the street had a bustling life of its own as well. Women stuck their heads out of windows six or seven storeys above it, and shouted down to their friends in the street. Children ran across it like rabbits, almost under the wheels of the sight-seeing buses, to disappear into some chosen courtyard and play their loud cheerful games. And workmen hammered away at the façades of some of the houses which were being restored, striding about unconcernedly along wobbly platforms on iron supports which concealed a whole block of buildings on one side of the street.

'About time too,' Will commented practically. 'Some of the houses look as if they'd fall down any minute.'

'I don't know.' Pat cocked an eye at them. 'Those stones look pretty strong. They've stood there a few hundred years, and I dare say they'll stand up for a few more.'

They had almost forgotten the Castle in the interest of the street leading to it. Now they moved slowly on, past a high tower with a notice outside which said this was the Outlook Tower and that a fine view of Edinburgh could be obtained from the Camera Obscura at the top, admission one shilling. The boys slowed up their steps, looking at one another.

'What's a Camera Obscura?' Will asked rather reluctantly. He did not like confessing to ignorance about anything that sounded vaguely scientific.

Pat had only a slightly clearer idea. 'I think they do it with lenses. You know, a sort of camera thing that reflects objects far away. I don't know if it's worth a shilling.'

Although Will had plenty of money in his pocket, he felt some delicacy about offering to pay for the two of them. Besides, it was the Castle they wanted to see. And presently, round the bed at the top of the steep street, they saw the wide Esplanade stretching out between them and the Castle drawbridge. It seemed to hang in the air above Princes Street Gardens far below, and after the crushed semi-darkness of the Royal Mile both boys found themselves drawing deep breaths of relief.

DUNGEONS AND JEWELS

Pat strolled over to examine the huge statue of Earl Haig reining his bronze horse in as though it might gallop right over the edge of the Esplanade. But Will had found another monument, and was reading the inscription which said it had been raised to the memory of Sergeant Ewart of the Greys, who won fame at the Battle of Waterloo by capturing single-handed, after a severe struggle, the eagle of Napoleon's prize regiment, the 45th Infantry. Just for a moment he wondered if Sergeant Ewart had had a hand-to-hand struggle with a large bird kept as the regiment's mascot. Then he remembered that Napoleon's eagles meant flags, and, allergic as he was towards history, he could not help feeling a little stirred by the exploit of the soldier whose monument lay still within sound of military bugles.

Awed in spite of themselves by the size of the fortress, they passed under the drawbridge, flanked on either side by the gigantic stone figures of William Wallace and Robert the Bruce, and began wandering past the inner buildings, through smaller courtyards, until they reached Argyll's Prison. Will had wanted to find a good dungeon, and now here one was. He shivered slightly as he looked down into the dark grim room beneath the tower, and felt some relief when Pat said they might as well go now and see the Crown jewels, adding that that sort of thing was more in Chris and Janet's line, but since they were here. . . .

They found the jewels sparkling on cushions inside an iron cage in the middle of a smallish room. Pat, who had seen the English Crown jewels in the Tower of London, was a little contemptuous at first, because there weren't many of them and they didn't make much of a blaze. But

THE HOUSE OF THE PELICAN

Will had, at this point, rather shamefacedly pulled out the guide which his mother had insisted upon his bringing with him, and which he had already consulted when looking at Argyll's Prison to see how many prisoners had been kept in it.

'D'you know,' he said, reading rapidly, 'that stone fellow, Robert the Bruce, actually wore the crown! I wonder how he got it on, on top of his helmet?'

'Just the circle bit . . .' Pat was looking over his shoulder at the book. 'They added those arches and things afterwards. And look, it says the Crown jewels were lost for over a hundred years! Found in an old box, where they'd been put when Scotland and England were joined together——'

'There's the box,' Will said with slight awe, pointing to an old oak chest with a notice on it, standing in a corner of the room. They imagined the old crown, set with its amethysts and pearls, along with the big heavy Sword of State and the long slim sceptre, jammed into the box, and Pat measured its length with his eye to make sure they would all go in. They would—just—and having satisfied himself of that, he followed Will (who had decided that he'd had enough history for today) out into the fresh air.

A cobbled way led through an ancient gateway towards the pinnacle of the great rock. Here, nearly five hundred feet above sea-level, was an open-paved space, containing the gun battery. The ancient cannon, Mons Meg, pointed her muzzle defiantly, as she had done for five hundred years, over the bastion towards the town. But there were modern cannon too, resting on their well-oiled gun-carriages, one of them marking the time for Edinburgh citizens by firing each day at one o'clock.

DUNGEONS AND JEWELS

Pat and Will went forward to the edge of the bastion and looked down. The great rock fell beneath them sheer as a cliff, to be merged in the gentle greenery of the Gardens below. People were strolling about, small as flies, and children played like dancing motes by the fountain and the bandstand a long way off. Farther off still the long line of Princes Street ran like a ribbon, and the rattle of its trams reached them faintly in the still morning air. And beyond that again, over the roofs of Edinburgh, they caught a blue glimpse of the Firth of Forth with the ships and the floating island of Inchcolm.

'Do you know what?' said Will after a minute or two, 'I'm going to like this place, even if it is historic.'

Pat did not answer. He was shying a small pebble down into the Gardens below. Will glanced at him.

'What's the matter?' he asked.

'I'm sick of new places,' Pat burst out; 'no matter how interesting they are. York was interesting, I suppose, and Manchester too, in its way. That's where the orchestra played last. Dad can't do anything else, I know, but trail Janet and me wherever he goes. But I do wish we had a home.'

Will felt both sorry and uncomfortable. Already this summer he had done a lot of travelling with his parents—Rome, Paris, London, and now Edinburgh. He tried to imagine what it would be like to go on travelling for ever, with only a boarding-school and rooms somewhere in London, in between. But the more he tried, the more he remembered the big white house with its spacious rooms waiting for him and his parents on the other side of the Atlantic; that and the little New England town of Fairport, near enough Boston for his father to commute by car every day, and big enough to have good times in with his friends.

'Can't your father get taken on by a resident orchestra?' he suggested. 'Then it would be worth while his renting a house and maybe engaging a housekeeper to look after Janet.'

Pat shook his head. 'We're not so keen on resident orchestras as you are in the States. Ours have to keep going on tour to make money.'

'Why, in my home town, Fairport, we've got a mighty good orchestra—pretty nearly as good as the Boston Symphony ! Father's on the committee. That's why we . . .' He stopped suddenly, as an idea flashed through his brain.

'Why you what?' A seagull, flying in from the Firth, swooped past Pat's ear as he spoke.

'Are you *sure* your father isn't a soloist ?' Will asked anxiously.

'No ; he's just a tenor trombone. Trombones don't play solos, or even concertos, though they do get a few bars of jam all to themselves with some of the composers—Wagner and Strauss, for example.'

'Now !' Will said reproachfully ; 'I thought you said you weren't musical !'

'I'm not, but I hear Dad talking about it, of course. This fellow Strauss—not the *Blue Danube* one, the one who uses a lot of brass—he wrote a symphony just before he died, and it's got quite a long bit in it for the tenor trombone. Only, Dad isn't going to get the chance of playing it. The first trombone's doing that.'

'D'you mean they're playing it at the Festival ?'

Pat nodded. 'It's coming on at the last concert. All

the critics are sitting with their mouths open, waiting to hear it. You see, everyone thought old Richard Strauss had shot his bolt, and he's been dead for some years anyway. But now they've found the score—he called it his Farewell Symphony—and it's going to have its first world performance here.'

'It's a terrible pity your father isn't at least playing that trombone solo bit!' Will remarked.

Pat looked at him in surprise, there was so much real regret in his tones. 'Why do you think it's such a pity?'

'Well . . .' the American hesitated, and then went on. 'As a matter of fact, the old man's come here specially to hear solo instrumentalists on behalf of the Fairport Orchestra. It needs fresh blood and a few new first-rate players. There's the nucleus back home, of course. But if only your father——'

'Yes, I know, don't say it,' Pat interrupted him rather bitterly. 'If Father hadn't been just a—a nucleus, he might have been chosen, and I suppose we could have really settled down and had a home in the States. As it is, if the Fairport Orchestra needs a trombonist, they'll invite Toscani. *He's* got the long juicy part in the Farewell Symphony, though actually Dad plays just as well as he does.'

'I'm sure of it,' Will said sympathetically.

Pat turned away from the bastion. 'It must be nearly one o'clock. That girl Chris has had Janet long enough on her hands already. I'll have to be getting back.'

The sightseers who had been swarming about the Castle had thinned out now. They passed over the drawbridge again and crossed the Esplanade, entering the narrow crooked street lined with its tall stone houses.

They had just drawn level with the Outlook Tower, and were saying to each other that it might be worth while looking into some day, when suddenly there came a shattering boom and roar behind them which made them both jump.

The one o'clock gun had gone off. Its echoes reverberated right down the street, thrown from one side to the other by the stone walls, which caught them and flung them back. A puff of white smoke floated above the bastion, then dispersed lazily into the blue sky above. While the boys were getting their breath again a stout Edinburgh citizen paused beside them, took out his watch calmly, and moved the minute-hand on.

'Five minutes slow,' they heard him mutter, putting it to his ear.

They waited till he had moved on again. Then Willington Bloomfield burst out laughing.

'For all the world like the White Rabbit in *Alice in Wonderland*!' he said.

Chapter V

A SEA-LION IN THE HOUSE

CHRIS always considered that after she had helped her mother to wash and dry the dishes after lunch she was free to do what she liked. Now, however, she was bound by her promise to Mr Foley to look after Janet, and also by her anxiety about what Janet might be up to if she left her alone in the house.

Pat went around with Will Bloomfield every day, and she envied them bitterly. As a matter of fact they would have been quite glad to take her along too, because she knew Edinburgh and they didn't. But they didn't want Janet 'tagging on', as Pat expressed it, and *somebody* had to take care of Janet.

Mr Foley left every morning to attend rehearsals of his orchestra. Most afternoons he stayed indoors because he was naturally tired, after playing all morning, and he knew he would have to play again at night. When he wasn't lying on top of his bed reading a detective novel or studying a new score, he was practising his trombone. He practised very softly, for fear of disturbing anyone, making dim sad sounds and sliding his arm down the long brass instrument.

Unfortunately there was an old lady in the room across the passage who did not care for trombones. She wrote a great many letters in her room, and the notes of the trombone made her punctuate them in all the wrong places. Whenever Mr Foley paused to take breath at the end of a phrase, or to give his arm a rest, the old lady became so flurried that she put full stops in the middle of her sentences, thus reducing them to nonsense.

She did not like to speak to Mr Foley about this, which would have been far the best thing to do. Instead, she quietly set about looking for some place else to stay in. By a piece of most unusual luck (because every hotel in the city was packed) she found friends who said she could come to them as a paying guest. So she told Mrs MacKendrick she was leaving, and Mrs MacKendrick was very upset.

'Right in the middle of the Festival too!' Mrs MacKendrick complained to Chris. 'When everyone's booked rooms already, and they all want to be nearer Princes Street anyhow!'

A SEA-LION IN THE HOUSE

'Don't worry,' Chris tried to soothe her, 'somebody's sure to turn up.'

'Carrying a trombone, of course!' sniffed her mother. 'Or maybe a trumpet this time. I wish Mr Foley and yon girl Janet of his—oh, well!' She was a kind-hearted woman really, and was sorry for the quiet tired man. 'They're decent folk anyway, and he has to do his practice, I suppose. But yon Janet'll end up on the stage.'

That gave Chris an idea, though she was a little chary of putting it before her mother. 'You—you wouldn't like putting up somebody from the Arden Company, would you? They're coming to the Lyceum next week, and they'll be sure to be looking for rooms. They're a *good* company—it's a Shakespeare play——'

'No theatricals,' her mother said firmly, 'not even if it's Scott they're acting in. Oh, I know fine, they're all respectable nowadays, but they want an early meal just the same. And then they come in late after the play, clamouring for supper.'

Chris sighed. It would have been fun having a real actor or actress staying here. Not one of the famous ones, of course. The famous ones would never put up with the mattresses. But somebody gay and pretty, who could tell interesting stories and be a change from the usual run of school teachers on holiday, old ladies with no homes and lots of complaints, and young bank clerks who made silly jokes. . . .

Mrs MacKendrick hung up a dish towel and put the last plate away in the cupboard. 'Some Edinburgh folk see less of the Festival than most,' she said rather bitterly. Then, as her daughter stood silent and thoughtful beside her, she realised that Chris wasn't having much fun either.

'You should go out and amuse yourself,' she added; 'it's a lovely day. Why not take Janet into the Gardens for a bit?'

'I've had enough of Janet this morning. Pat's asked me to go out with him and his friend. He says he's an American and quite nice. They want me to show them some interesting places.'

'What about going to the Zoo? Then Janet can come with you. She'd enjoy seeing the animals.'

Chris sighed again. Of course it was up to Pat to take charge of his sister during the afternoons, but she had hoped they might have shaken off Janet and left her behind in Mrs MacKendrick's charge. However, her mother told her firmly that she could not take Janet out herself, and that the lassie needed some fresh air. Chris ran off to tell Pat, who agreed resignedly, and Janet was told to put on her coat and come with them to see the animals in the Zoo.

Janet was delighted. She had played at being housemaid all morning and was thoroughly tired of the game. She scrambled into her best coat, a bright cherry-red one with a little red cap to match, and they started off. Will Bloomfield had promised to meet Pat at the corner of Princes Street at three o'clock. His face fell when he saw the two girls, but he did his best to be agreeable, and cheered up at the suggestion of visiting the Zoo.

They got on to a tram with TO THE ZOO marked up in front of it, and had quite a long drive. In spite of all the culture there was in Edinburgh at the moment, a surprising number of people seemed to have chosen to watch the wild animals in the Zoo park instead. People were streaming through the gates, the restaurant was crowded already with early tea-drinkers, and the roar of the lions mingled with

A SEA-LION IN THE HOUSE

the chatter of the crowds as they visited one place after another.

Janet became so interested that she was not any trouble at all. The pelicans fascinated her, with their long clattering beaks, and she asked their names. Will told her they were called Jelly-cans, and she was very annoyed when the other two burst out laughing, and insisted upon practising 'Pelican' two or three times, to make sure she pronounced it properly. Then they went on to the big pond where the sea-lions splashed about or sat on rocks, whiskered and melancholy.

Here there were fewer people because it was not yet feeding-time. The boys walked round to the other end of the pond, with Janet tagging along between them. But Chris, who had been running about the house sweeping and dusting all morning, felt her legs give way under her after the amount of walking they had done already. She plumped down on a seat, just where she was. And that was how she came to meet the Bonds.

They were sitting farther along the seat, watching the nearest sea-lion intently. Mr Bond was a short fat man whose little legs hardly touched the ground. Mrs Bond was very like him, which was curious as they were not related, except by marriage. She was perhaps a little fatter, but very quietly dressed, with a round red face like his.

'Watch out, Father!' she said suddenly. 'He's going to give tongue.'

Chris, who had scarcely noticed them, started and stared. What a very odd thing to say! Mr Bond paid no attention but went on staring straight in front of him with his hands on his knees. However, his eyes seemed to bulge slightly, and, following the direction of his stare, she saw it was fixed upon a grizzled sea-lion who had suddenly reared itself up on the rock it was sitting on, and was blowing its whiskers out. The next moment it had begun to bark, very hoarsely and sharply.

Mr Bond leaned forward and cleared his throat.

Mrs Bond spoke again, just as sharply as the sea-lion. ' No, not here,' she said.

Mr Bond swivelled his head round and fixed his eyes upon Chris instead. ' Funny beasts, sea-lions,' he said.

As he seemed to be addressing her, Chris answered at once. ' Yes, but there are funnier beasts still. Have you seen the orang-outang ? '

' We're just interested in sea-lions,' Mr Bond replied. He had half-closed his eyes now and seemed to fall into a doze. ' Studying 'em,' he said, with his eyes still shut.

' Do you mean to say you haven't bothered about the polar bears or the monkeys or anything ? ' Chris was quite astonished. It seemed such a waste of two admission tickets.

Mrs Bond seemed to want to change the subject. ' Do you belong to Edinburgh yourself ? ' she asked. She had a pleasanter voice than her husband's, but there was something rather nice as well as odd about them both.

Chris said she did. Mrs Bond looked pleased for some reason or other, and leaned towards her confidentially : ' Then perhaps you can tell us something. We've just arrived in Edinburgh this morning, and find every hole and corner full. I suppose you couldn't recommend a hotel ? '

' A cheap hotel,' Mr Bond put in firmly, opening his eyes, ' 'cos we're not made of money, y' know.'

They were sitting farther along the seat

'Yes, I do.' Chris spoke rapidly, seizing her chance all the more quickly because the Bonds interested her so much and she wanted to see more of them. 'My mother keeps a guest-house and we've got a room free. It's—it's not very near the centre of the town, but then it's not expensive either, and you can't have everything.'

'Indeed you can't,' agreed Mrs Bond, 'and I'm sure any place belonging to the mother of a girl like you would be nice and clean. What do you think, Father? Shall we let Miss . . . here show us the room?'

A gleam of caution descended upon Chris. Letting the rooms to Mr Foley hadn't exactly been a success, on account of the trombone, though of course her mother liked the Foleys otherwise, and wouldn't dream of asking them to leave. Still, one must be careful not to make another mistake.

'I'm afraid Mother won't have anyone Theatrical,' she said, although she felt it quite unnecessary, because of the Bonds' appearance. 'You're not on the stage, are you?'

Rather an odd look passed between Mr and Mrs Bond. But Mrs Bond said quickly, 'Oh, no, we're not on the stage. Are we, Father?'

'Certainly not,' said Mr Bond. 'No, we're not on the stage. Are we, Mother?' His own moustache, which was very like the sea-lion's, began to twitch as though he wanted to laugh. The sleek animal on the rock raised itself and gave another hoarse bark. Mr Bond swallowed in his throat.

'Tell you what, dearie,' said Mrs Bond: 'you give us the address of that boarding house of yours, and we'll turn up and speak to your mother when we've finished here.

Then, if everything's satisfactory, Father and I can fetch our luggage from the station and move in tonight.'

Chris gave them the address and got up from the seat. The others were waving her to join them anyway. She felt that she would like them to meet the Bonds too. Perhaps Pat might help her to judge what they would be like in the house.

'Janet—that's the little girl over there—wants to see the giraffe. Would you like to come with us?' she asked.

Mr Bond shook his head. 'Thanks. Not interested in anything except the sea-lions,' he said. 'Studying 'em,' he said again as he nodded goodbye.

She told the others about what she had done, as they wandered about in search of the giraffes. 'What, that funny little pair?' Pat had noticed them from across the pond. 'Bet you they don't turn up.'

Will looked envious. 'If I were here on my own, I'd change to your place like winking. I'm sick of big hotels where you never meet anyone, and I'd sure like to know a man who spends all his time studying sea-lions. You don't think he's crazy, do you?'

Chris shook her head. 'It sounds daft, but I'm sure he isn't. I feel somehow as if he had a *reason* for studying them, though I can't think what it is.'

They had come some distance from the pond already, but Pat, looking over his shoulder, could still catch a glimpse of the two squat figures sitting, oddly motionless, on their seat. 'Perhaps he's a professor of zoology or whatever they call it. He may be meaning to write a book about sea-lions.'

But Chris didn't think it likely that Mr Bond could be

A SEA-LION IN THE HOUSE

a professor of anything. There were a great many professors in Edinburgh, which is a university city, but none of them was the least like Mr Bond.

After they had looked at the giraffes, they went to the restaurant and had tea. This was Will Bloomfield's idea, and he gave them a splendid tea, with ices to finish. Then they took the tram back into the centre of the city, and parted. They had spent some time over their tea, because when Chris and the Foleys returned to Number Seven they heard that the Bonds had called there already and taken their room.

'They'll be here for supper,' Mrs MacKendrick told Chris; adding doubtfully, 'they look very quiet and respectable, but I hope you haven't done anything rash.'

Everyone sat round the same big long table in the dining-room and talked to everyone else. Mrs Bond had changed for the meal, which pleased Mrs MacKendrick, who liked her guests to take a little trouble to look nice. The little square woman now wore a very shiny black satin dress and three strings of artificial pearls wound round the place where her neck should be. But her hair was scraped back from her face and she still looked respectable in spite of the pearls.

Mr Bond was polite and attentive about passing plates, but he said little more than he had said at the Zoo. To make up for this, Mrs Bond talked a lot, in her fat jolly voice. She got on very well with Mr Foley, who talked too, more than usual. Mr Foley had toured the Continent in his youth, playing in an orchestra that had foreign engagements. He and Mrs Bond talked about Paris and Brussels, and the places to stay in there, and the way the Italians cook spaghetti, until Mrs MacKendrick felt quite proud of such travelled conversation taking place at her table.

But still, she wondered a little. The Bonds didn't seem people to have much money for travel. The two young school teachers who were staying in the house were greatly impressed. 'What a lot you've seen, Mr Bond!' one of them exclaimed. 'Were you and Mrs Bond studying anything when you were abroad?'

Chris quite expected him to say they were studying sea-lions, but instead, for some reason, Mr Bond looked a little put-out, and his wife as usual came to the rescue. 'Well, you can't help picking up a few things when you go around,' she remarked, with her eyes on Janet, who suddenly gave a great yawn.

The meal was over, and people had only lingered to hear the talk between Mrs Bond and Mr Foley. Now Mrs Bond said, 'That child's asleep in her seat! Who puts you to bed, dearie? I'll tuck you up if you like.'

Mr Foley's orchestra was not playing that night, as it happened, but he was grateful for the offer, and accepted it at once as he very much wanted to go out and hear someone else's playing. Chris was equally glad that someone else was willing to put Janet to bed. So Mrs Bond left the room with Janet, and ran her bath-water for her, and told her about the lovely embroidered dresses the little girls wore in Paris, and tucked her up, kissed her goodnight, and left her in her little room under the skylight window.

By that time Chris and Mrs MacKendrick had finished washing up the supper dishes together. Then Mrs MacKendrick took some sewing, and Chris a book that she wanted to finish, and they went upstairs to the great

A SEA-LION IN THE HOUSE

cold drawing-room, where the other guests who were not out at concerts were sitting around. Pat played bezique with one of the school teachers, and everyone felt a little dreary at not being out enjoying themselves under the lights of Princes Street, but one can't buy tickets for things every night of the week.

The Bonds went to their room early because they said they were tired. Mr Foley came in quietly just about ten o'clock, and Mrs MacKendrick made cups of cocoa for everyone. The long northern light had lingered so that she had not troubled to draw the curtains, and now the sky showed greenish-blue, filling the darkened window panes.

Everyone was tired with sight-seeing or housework, but somehow the room, with its blurred outlines and shadows, held them. Now, very faintly, came the *boom-boom* of the cannons fired at the end of the Military Tattoo, which showed it was eleven o'clock. The school teachers were just saying how they meant to go and see it tomorrow, and Pat was urging his father to let him go too, when the drawing-room door suddenly burst open.

There stood Janet in her nightdress. Her eyes were fevered and bright, and her voice shook as she said, ' I can't sleep, I'm frightened ! There's a sea-lion in the house——'

' Good gracious, Janet ! ' said Mr Foley.

' Don't tell such tales, just to make a sensation,' Pat told her sharply ; ' you know there isn't any such thing.'

' But there is ! ' Janet began to shout. ' First it looked at me through that little window in the roof—I could see its horrid whiskers quite plainly. And then it got in somehow, and it's barking all over the house ! '

THE HOUSE OF THE PELICAN

Mrs MacKendrick went firmly towards her. 'Come away and I'll put you in bed again. I'll sort the sea-lions!'

Everyone looked very relieved, especially Mr Foley. Mrs MacKendrick took Janet's hand and led her upstairs again. Curiously enough the child seemed really frightened. Her hand was quite cold. Still, Mrs MacKendrick didn't intend to stand any nonsense, and she knew Janet's facility for making up stories by now. It was high time the child learned the difference between truth and falsehood, at nine years old!

She led her very quietly past the Bonds' room just opposite Janet's, and did not speak for fear of disturbing them until she had safely closed the door of the little room under the eaves. Then, while Janet scrambled under the blankets again, she spoke to her very severely.

'Babies make up fairy stories, but you're not a baby,' she said, 'and if you go on making them up, now you're a big girl, soon nobody will believe a word you say. It's all very well to invent stories in your head, but it's cheating to tell them to other people.'

'There *was* a sea-lion,' Janet said sulkily.

'Just get out of bed again, and put on your wee dressing-gown,' Mrs MacKendrick told her briskly; adding, 'I don't want you to take cold.'

Janet was so surprised she did what she was told at once. Mrs MacKendrick pushed a chair under the skylight window, poking the little glass open as far as it would go. 'Now climb up there and put your head out,' she ordered.

Janet did so.

'Do you see any sea-lions?'

A SEA-LION IN THE HOUSE

'Not now,' Janet still spoke sulkily; 'it'll have slid off.'

Mrs MacKendrick didn't say anything. She just looked very sad as she tucked the bedclothes round Janet again, and then began to move towards the door. Suddenly Janet called after her in quite a different voice, rather a muffled one as if a piece of blanket had got into her mouth.

'I'm not a baby. I—I expect the roof's too steep for a sea-lion to climb anyway.'

Mrs MacKendrick went back and kissed her. 'That's a good lassie! Now, you didn't see one after all, did you?'

'No.' The voice under the blankets was just a whisper.

'You're getting real grown-up, learning to tell truth from stories. That's the first thing grown-up folk have to learn. Now go to sleep, dearie, and don't be dreaming about hearing sea-lions barking, or Chris'll never take you to the Zoo——'

Next moment she was sorry she had said it. For Janet suddenly sat up, her eyes dilated. 'But I *did* hear one! Listen! It's barking now. . . .'

In spite of herself Mrs MacKendrick stiffened, standing still in the middle of the dark little room. Janet had startled her into listening. But now nothing came to them but the stillness of the night and the slow ticking of the grandfather clock on the landing.

'I thought you were going to be a good girl and tell the truth,' she said angrily. 'I'm real disappointed with you, Janet.'

Without saying any more goodnights she shut the door and went downstairs again. Mr Foley had been waiting to thank her and to mumble some apologies for his daughter. 'I really don't know what to do about Janet's habit of making up stories,' he said, passing a hand distractedly over his hair; 'she *must* be broken of it. And the trouble is, strangers sometimes believe her——'

'I can imagine that,' Mrs MacKendrick said dryly, 'seeing she seemed to believe them herself. She confessed in the end that she hadn't seen anything through the window. And then, just when I thought she was quieted, up she sat and said she could hear a sea-lion bark. And just for the minute I thought I heard it myself!'

Chapter VI

THE OUTLOOK TOWER

It was a beautiful afternoon and blazingly hot, as happens sometimes in Scotland right at the end of the summer. Princes Street—the most beautiful shopping street in Europe—was thronged with tourists from all over the world, and above the clamour and noise of their passage came faintly, from the Gardens bordering the whole length of the street, the skirl and whine of bagpipes. There was an open-air stage in the middle of the Gardens, and on the stage a troupe of girl dancers were performing a reel, before a fascinated audience sitting on chairs in front of them.

The Foleys, Will Bloomfield and Chris watched for nothing, behind the chairs which cost money to sit on. Again, Will would have gladly paid for them all, but the others seemed to take it for granted that one was a fool to pay for what one could see and hear for nothing. So he stood, shifting from one foot to another and thinking how the medals the girls wore looked exactly like fish scales.

They were quite little girls, and they danced with fixed set smiles, twirling and kicking till the big silver buckles on their shoes winked in the sun. Janet heaved a deep sigh as the dance came to a close. Her brother interpreted the sigh correctly.

'You'll never do that in a thousand years, no matter how long you practise in front of the mirror,' he said.

'I could if I had a hat with a feather and a tartan thing over my shoulders,' she answered indignantly.

'Do you want to see the Floral Clock?' asked Chris. 'I've just time to take you there if you like.'

The Floral Clock lay farther on, at the end of the Gardens, quite close to the railings separating it from the steep street going up towards the Castle. Now that the pipes had stopped a lot of other people had the same idea, and they had some difficulty in keeping together because of the crowd. At last they came in sight of the big green bank with the gigantic clock marked out on it in flowers. Small bright plants had been sunk into metal cases shaped like Roman numerals, and the big flowery hands even pointed to the correct time.

'A quarter past four.' Will glanced at the clock above the North British hotel to make sure. 'I suppose there's some mechanism under the turf that makes the hands move.'

'It's worked by electricity,' Chris was saying, when suddenly Janet darted away from them towards the railings. Chris ran after her and brought her back, afraid she might lose her in the crowd. But Janet kept twisting backwards to catch another glimpse of the stalwart fishwife who had just passed the end of the Gardens and was making her way up the Mound.

'Let me go, Chris! It's Effie—Effie the fishwife, and she promised to take me home for tea!'

'She doesn't want you for tea today. I bet she hasn't sold all her fish yet—she's still got the creel on her back. Oh, do shut up, Janet! She'll be coming round to us next week, and you can talk to her then.'

Chris cast another rather hurried glance at the clock. She said to the boys, 'I've got to go home now, I promised Mother I'd be back at five.'

'All right. Take Janet, won't you? She may as well go too.'

'Why should I? I've had her all morning——'

Just then a whole bunch of people newly off a sight-seeing bus entered the Gardens by the little gate in the railings and pressed forward to see the clock. Someone jostled against Chris, separating her from the others. There was no point in trying to find them again, when she had already said she was going home. Congratulating herself upon having landed the boys with Janet, she walked away quickly towards the dance platform again, and the exit which would bring her out opposite the right tram stop.

The boys turned away from the clock and went through the little gate leading on to the Mound. Effie had passed out of sight, and in any case so many people were going up and down the steep hill that it was impossible to pick anyone out.

THE HOUSE OF THE PELICAN

'Let's go that way again,' Pat suggested; adding, 'we might as well have a look at the Camera Obscura thing in that tower. I dare say it's worth a bob after all.'

Greatly relieved at not having had Janet foisted on them, they sauntered along, and finally found themselves once more on the Royal Mile. The dark archways between the tall houses looked interesting, and they stopped to explore one or two on the way. The old courtyards beyond them seemed to house numerous families, and were ringed round with dark entries leading to twisty corkscrew staircases. Sometimes only a scrap of sky was visible above the turrets and gables surrounding the yards. From little windows high up, strings of washing hung like pennants, strung along a wooden projecting frame with a rope-pulley to haul them out or in.

'Gosh! What a way of drying the laundry!' Will exclaimed, looking up at a fluttering row of garments.

'Even if there *was* a drying green, I wouldn't care about carrying a washing basket up and down all those stairs,' Pat said, as they left the last courtyard and proceeded towards the Outlook Tower.

There were enough stairs here too, but presently they arrived, puffing, at the top of the tower. Here a flat roof-garden had been made, and once more they seemed to hang in the air high above the city, with the blue waters of the Firth beyond. A few other people were lounging about, too, waiting for the attendant to summon them into the room with the Camera Obscura. At last the party who were filling up the room already came out, and Pat and Will filed in with the next lot of people to see what the room contained.

It was so shadowy that at first they could hardly see.

THE OUTLOOK TOWER

The whole floor of the room seemed to be taken up by an immense sort of white table, ringed round by a circular gallery a few feet above it. Everyone stepped up on to the gallery and stood in a circle about the table. The attendant closed the doors and darkened the room still further. And then, miraculously, the big white table began to be splashed with colour; the grey of the stone houses, the green of the gardens, and the blue of the sky above. Pat and Will craned forward excitedly, looking down at a little vision of Edinburgh brought close to them as if the Outlook Tower itself were some sort of gigantic telescope. . . .

'Look at the trams!' exclaimed Will, pointing. Although they were so far from Princes Street, they seemed to be looking right down into it: a very small street, of course, with midget trams riding up and down it, and people getting on and off like flies. But the party was told to keep moving, and as the boys edged slowly round the big table, they kept getting another point of view. Now it was the slope of the Mound, and a black cluster, like a swarm, at the corner of the Gardens nearest to it, where people still milled round the Floral Clock.

They moved on again. Now they were looking right down the Royal Mile, and because the picture was nearer and clearer, they could make out the people quite distinctly. They even saw a fishwife, slanted forward with the weight of the creel on her back, come out of one of the dark entries and walk down towards the Mound.

'It's dashed like that woman Janet pointed out,' Pat muttered, ' but of course fishwives all dress the same, with those bunchy skirts, so it mayn't be. . . .'

The fishwife mingled with the crowd farther down,

and became lost to view. Outside, the sun shone so strongly that the great lenses of the Camera Obscura caught and sharpened the smallest detail, so that the boys even saw a ball roll out of the mouth of the archway from which the fishwife had emerged, and lie on the pavement outside it. A bunch of children ran out after it, caught it up and threw it to one another until it landed on the roadway, and a passing car had to swerve to avoid knocking down a little girl who had plunged after the ball.

The little girl was wearing a bright red coat and a red cap set sideways on her dark hair. Will heard Pat draw in his breath sharply. 'That's Janet!' he said.

'It can't be,' Will said; 'she went home with Chris, didn't she?'

'I don't know—I thought she was going to, but then she'd caught sight of this Effie, and was dead set on following her up the Mound. Suppose—suppose she'd got away from Chris and followed her after all?'

THE OUTLOOK TOWER

They almost fell over the edge of the railing above the big table, straining for another glimpse of the girl in the red coat. But she and the other children had disappeared through the entry again and were no doubt playing in the courtyard within.

'We'd better go and see,' Pat said abruptly, leaving the rail. Will followed him out of the room, and for a few moments the increased light dazzled their eyes so that they had almost to feel their way down the stairs of the Outlook Tower. The entry they were seeking was a little way farther down the street, on the opposite side of the road. Pat had marked it quite easily, because it stood next to the scaffolding which completely hid the frontages of the two houses on the farther side of it. They crossed the road and plunged into the dark roofed-in tunnel. As they did, they heard the sound of singing somewhere beyond.

Now they had entered a little stone-paved courtyard, surrounded by ancient gables. Some children were playing with the ball in the courtyard, while streams of washing flapped lazily high above their heads. They were playing a queer old game of their own, standing in a circle round one of their number and throwing the ball from hand to hand. As they threw it they sang words as old and queer as the game:

> '*The wind, the wind, the wind blows high,*
> *The snow comes tumbling from the sky,*
> *And Janet Foley's going to die*
> *For want of the golden city.*'

At the last word, the child who held the ball threw it straight at the one in the middle of the circle, who caught it and flung it back. Then the circle broke up momentarily, and a little girl, who had been hidden by it, ran out laughing. It was Janet.

'Come here at once!' Pat ordered through set teeth. 'I want you.'

Janet looked startled and cross. 'I'm not coming. I want to go on playing The Golden City.'

Pat stepped forward and grabbed her rather roughly. 'You're not going to do anything of the kind. You're going straight home.'

An older girl with squint teeth and very untidy hair called out, 'Aw, leave the kid alone, she's a right wee sport!'

The boys began marching her back across the yard, towards the street. They heard some shouts and rude remarks behind them, but paid no attention. By the time they had gone through the entry again, the ring had been formed once more, with the squint-toothed girl in the middle. And the singing followed them faintly as they reached the pavement outside.'

'... *comes tumbling from the sky,*
And Maisie Paterson's going to die
For want of the golden city.'

Janet had started crying. She cried very picturesquely, refusing to dry her tears on the handkerchief Will held out, in case it should make her nose red. All the same, the boys were deeply embarrassed at having to lead a sobbing child through the crowded street.

'What possessed you to run away from Chris like that?' Pat still spoke roughly because he had been greatly alarmed to find his sister in such a squalid place, and he knew she could never have found her way home alone.

They were playing a queer old game

'I didn't run away from Chris. I ran after Effie,' sniffed Janet.

'Then why didn't you stay with Effie? *She* knew where you lived. She'd have taken you home.'

'I ran after her like anything, but she was always in front. Besides, I didn't want her to take me home, I wanted to see where she was going. She went into such a funny old house—at least, she went under it 'cos it was built out over the street somehow, and it had a stone bird over the door, a—a jellycan like we saw at the Zoo——'

'She means a pelican,' Will said; adding, 'I guess there may be one too, carved in stone. Remember those old carvings we saw above some of the entries?'

Janet stopped sniffing, encouraged by their interest. She now began to enjoy herself telling her story. 'Well, I kept a little behind Effie in case she would take me home. So she went past the jel- pelican, into a funny little yard with a wooden staircase all crumbly and rotten. And she went up the staircase and knocked at a little wooden door high up somewhere in a roof that looked as if it was tumbling down.'

The boys glanced at each other over her head. Still, so far, her story might be possible.

'Go on. What happened next?' Pat asked.

'The door opened and a hand came out. I think it had money in it, because Effie took something and put it in her pocket. Then she brought out a big fish from her basket and the hand took it by the tail, and then the door closed. Oh, I forgot. There were millions of fish tails lying about the yard. Fish tails and fins and an awful smell——'

'There you are,' Pat said disgustedly to Will; 'she's just making up another story.'

Janet wasn't Will's sister, so he was merely amused. 'Didn't Effie see you when she came down the staircase again?' he asked.

Janet shook her head. 'She would have, but there were two big enormous ash-bins, and I hid behind them till she went away again. But I wanted to see what belonged to the hand, so after she'd gone I climbed the little staircase myself. One step was quite broken, and I nearly fell through——'

'Look here, Will,' Pat said sharply, 'I do wish you wouldn't encourage her to tell all these lies. Listening like that just makes her go on with them.'

The long afternoon had made them both rather hot and cross. 'I'm not encouraging her,' Will answered equally sharply, 'but I can ask some questions, can't I?'

'And I'm *not* telling lies!' Janet turned a furious face towards her brother. 'I *did* go up the little staircase, and I knocked on the door. And it opened, and there was a room full of things, with an old man who said I could come in if there wasn't anybody else with me——'

'What sort of things was the room full of?' Will asked, more to tease Pat than for anything else.

'Oh, lots of things.' Janet became vague. 'The room was too dark to see them properly. But I saw a little yellow box—he showed me that. It had a bird on the lid, and when you touched something, the bird began singing.'

'You're not being the least bit funny,' Pat told her coldly, 'and if you go on inventing sea-lions and yellow boxes, you'll just be sent back to London. That's what will happen to *you*.'

'Now *you're* not telling the truth!' Janet exclaimed triumphantly. 'You know quite well I can't go back to

THE OUTLOOK TOWER

London till you and Father take me. Mrs Browning's gone on holiday and the house is shut up.'

Mrs Browning was their London landlady. For some reason or other, Pat grew suddenly furious with both Will and Janet. They had reached the top of the Mound, and he saw approaching them the tram which would take them home.

'Here's the tram—hurry up or we'll lose it. Will can walk back to his hotel, it's near enough. Unless he thinks it's worth while taking a taxi.'

Will knew quite well that Pat was angry with him because he had drawn Janet out and made her tell more stories just for the fun of it. But he wasn't going to apologise, and indeed a spirit of mischief made him call after them, ' You must take me to see the house with the pelican, Janet ! Give me a date some time ! '

Chapter VII

TEACHING JANET A LESSON

MRS BLOOMFIELD, unlike most American women, preferred to have her breakfast downstairs. In hotels, she even had it with her hat on, so that not a minute was wasted in dressing to go out and learn something immediately afterwards. Her husband always felt taciturn in the mornings, so erected a barrier of newspaper, thus leaving Mrs Bloomfield to concentrate upon Willington.

Mrs Bloomfield's bright birdlike glances dwelt upon all the other breakfasters in turn. This was a great hotel for celebrities to stay in, and she liked celebrities, so long as they were really cultured and not just beauty queens or merely excessively rich. The large illustrated brochure of the Festival contained photographs of many of the visiting stars. She had it on her lap, and would consult it now and then, to see if anybody looked like one of the photographs.

'Don't look round, Willington,' she said suddenly, 'but there's Toscani just sitting down! The man giving the order to that waiter.'

Mr Bloomfield spoke from behind his newspaper. 'If he's got any sense he won't order coffee. I must say I shall be glad to taste real coffee again.'

'Who's Toscani?' Will tried to sound interested.

'Well, I guess it's natural that you wouldn't know, seeing he isn't a prominent soloist, except in his own line. But he's playing the part for solo trombone in the new Strauss symphony. Your father just can't wait to hear it.'

TEACHING JANET A LESSON

'That who he is?' Mr Bloomfield lowered his paper an inch to take a look at the trombone player. 'I must say, Hannah, you have a remarkable memory for names. How did you spot the fellow?'

'Well, this brochure has a picture of the players in the New English Orchestra. I spotted him from that.' Mrs Bloomfield sounded modestly pleased by her success.

'The New English Orchestra?' Will remembered that was the name of the one Pat's father was playing in. 'I say, I know one of the players—at least, he's Pat Foley's father, though I haven't met him yet. Pat feels a bit sore that he isn't playing the solo part instead of that fellow, Toscanini.'

'*Willington!*' His mother sounded shocked. 'You know perfectly well Toscanini isn't a trombone player. I said Toscani.'

'Let's be thankful that Willington has at least heard of Toscanini before,' Mr Bloomfield said. 'As for this fellow, Pat Foley, that you've been going around with, Willington, he seems a nice straight-forward lad. Don't you feel you would like to entertain him in some way or other?'

Will looked a little uncertain. Since parting so hurriedly a few days before, he and Pat had held no communication with each other. They had had no time to fix another rendezvous, even if Pat wanted one, and Will had an uneasy feeling that Pat was annoyed with him for taking Janet's part during the argument which had occurred then.

But his mother was making kindly plans already. 'You know we're going to drive out and see that old castle this afternoon. It's open to the public, and the

Guide says it's a pure gem of Adam architecture with a wing in Scots seventeenth-century style. I adore Adam architecture. Why not ask your friend to come with us?'

It might be a good idea, at that. But one had to be sure. 'Do they serve teas?' Will asked practically.

'Dear me, you're getting quite British. Yes, they apparently do. It says "Refreshments served in the Ballroom".'

'Oh, I wouldn't bother about that, but Pat likes his tea.'

'Then call him up and ask him.'

But Will didn't want to risk a cold refusal over the telephone. 'I might go round and see him this morning. Then I could find out if there was anything else he would prefer.'

'All right, but remember, Willington, I want you to come with us to this lovely old place—what's its name? —Drumfingal. So if he can't come, you'll just have to meet him another day. You must get a good grasp of architecture, it's very important.'

So Will went straight out after breakfast and caught a tram of the same number as that which Pat and Janet had taken. He knew their address too, and presently found himself walking along Caroline Square. It was just a week since Effie the fishwife had made her visit to the Square, and there she was again, walking slowly past the houses which didn't give her custom, and disappearing down the areas of those who did.

The door of Number Seven was opened by Chris, who told him to wait in the hall till she went and fetched Pat. Will was greatly relieved to find Pat just as friendly as ever in his quiet British way, and that he seemed pleased

TEACHING JANET A LESSON

by the afternoon's invitation, though Will thought it only fair to warn him that there would be 'a lot of history in it'.

'So long as it isn't a high-brow concert,' Pat said; adding, 'I did promise to nursemaid Janet in the afternoons, but if I look after her this morning instead, I dare say Chris will take her over.'

'Don't think I believed that tale of hers either,' Will said rather sheepishly. 'I only pretended to, so as to draw her out.'

Pat hastened to accept the implied apology. 'Oh, some bits would be true enough. That's the trouble with Janet, she starts off all right, and then she puts knobs on to her stories. All kids do it, but she hasn't grown out of the habit.'

'Why, I guess that bit about following Effie would be right enough, and she just went on from there. By the way, Effie's somewhere around. I met her as I came here.'

They were interrupted by Mr and Mrs Bond passing on their way out. Mr Bond said, 'Morning, my lads,' but Mrs Bond just gave her broad, fat smile.

When the hall door had closed on them, Pat, who had been thinking, said, 'I've half a mind to ask Effie if such a place even exists. You know, the one Janet said had a stone pelican above the door——'

'It might, you know,' Will pointed out, 'because most of the doorways have crests and things carved on them.'

'I don't believe it. I think Janet just remembered the pelicans at the Zoo, and stuck one on. If Effie says there's no such place, then I can give Janet a proper talking-to. I wonder if Effie's still in the Square?'

They went out on to the steps and saw her just climbing up from the area beneath them. She had a fat jolly face like Mrs Bond's, but she was a much bigger woman, and her eyes were keen and intelligent. 'Good mornin' to ye!' she said; 'and how d'ye like our town?'

'Very much, thanks,' Pat replied, 'in spite of nearly losing my sister the other day. She tells me she followed you right up the Mound.'

'Did she? The wee soul would be thinkin' on yon invitation to tea I gave her. Well, I never saw her, or I

TEACHING JANET A LESSON

wad have sent her home quick enough. Lassies shouldna' be wanderin' about in crowds.'

Will took a step or two forward. 'She said she followed you through an entry with a stone pelican carved above it, and that there was a wooden stairway in the court beyond, with a door at the top. Is that right?'

'Janet makes up such stories sometimes,' Pat interrupted apologetically; 'we wanted to know if there was any truth in this one.'

A tiny change had taken place in Effie's expression. Something leaped up in her eyes. But she only said, 'And whit, now, wad a pelican be?'

'It's a bird with a big beak.'

'I ken a lot o' birds, but there's none wi' an outlandish name like yon flyin' aboot Leith. Na! I dinna ken onything aboot pelicans. But I ken that wee lassies should be taught to speak the truth. Good mornin' to ye!' And she picked up the creel which had been resting on the step, and went down the Square again.

'So that's that,' said Will.

Pat was looking angry again. 'I wish Effie had spoken before Janet. She's got to be *shown* that the things she makes up don't exist. I tell you what: if you're not doing anything this morning, let's take her up the Royal Mile and ask her to point out the place!'

Will thought they might as well do that as anything else, though it was a pity to have Janet tagged on. However, Pat went to fetch Janet and brought her down. 'She insists that she can still lead us straight to the house,' her brother said, 'but we'll see.'

Although the sun shone so brightly over the wide streets and open squares of the city, it cast shadows over the Royal Mile. The day felt even a little cold as they began to walk up the steep bit towards the Castle. 'Take your time,' Pat told his little sister grimly; 'be sure we don't pass the house with the pelican. Perhaps there'll be a fish-tail or something lying just under it to mark the place.'

'You don't believe me, but I did see it!' Janet answered indignantly, and then became very quiet and intent, studying the stone lintels of every old house they passed.

She was so obviously searching for it that Will, at least, became convinced the stone pelican must be there after all. Pat, who knew his sister better, was not so sure. He knew how often she ended up by believing her own stories, because they had become vivid and real in her mind. He determined not to be cross with her, but to use this occasion as an object-lesson against imagining things too hard.

Once or twice Janet hesitated, as though she had found the right entry. But when they looked up there was no pelican there. When they reached the big hoarding with its three platforms, one above the other, supported on iron pillars, she brightened up and exclaimed, 'It was just beside this!'

The boys looked at each other. They remembered the little figure glimpsed in the Camera Obscura, running after the ball. Certainly it, and the other children, had appeared quite close to the scaffolding, so perhaps . . .

They almost ran past the place, just swerving in time to avoid a workman wheeling a barrow along the bit of paving under the iron supports. Sure enough, there was an archway under a tall grey house whose dusty windows facing the street showed that it was six storeys

TEACHING JANET A LESSON

high. The archway was more like a short tunnel, and it obviously led to a courtyard beyond.

'This is it!' Janet cried triumphantly, and then looked up.

There was an ancient shield, with a coronet carved above it, but no pelican.

'What did I tell you?' Pat turned to Will, shrugging his shoulders.

Janet stood stockstill, looking puzzled. 'I know!' she said suddenly. 'I didn't go *in* there, I went in somewhere else, where the pelican was!'

'Don't start making up things to cover yourself,' Pat told her sharply; 'we were in the tower opposite, looking down a sort of telescope, and we saw you run out of that very archway. Didn't we, Will?'

A tear began to trickle down Janet's face. She stamped her foot at her brother. 'Don't look at me like that! I followed Effie into that yard place, not this one, but the one with the pelican over the door. A lot of children came into it after she'd gone, and they threw a ball at me. I played with them, and we ran through a passage and came out here. We did!'

'I don't doubt that you came out here, but farther up there are only a few shops and then the castle. So just you come along and find the entrance. You know jolly well there isn't one.'

And there wasn't. Not one with a pelican above it anyway, although a dark alley or two divided the shops. By now Janet was crying freely. Will felt sorry for her. 'I say, old man'—he had an idea—'what about the houses behind all that scaffolding? Maybe there's an entrance there that we didn't see.'

THE HOUSE OF THE PELICAN

So they went back to look. But the hoarding stretched solidly over the façades of the two old houses that were having their frontages repaired, and there was only one little door to let the workmen through it with their barrows and things. It stood open now, showing that no entry led in anywhere between the two houses, nor did the stonework visible bear any sign of a sculptured pelican.

To make dead sure there could be no mistake Pat stopped a man who was loading a barrow with old stones. 'I suppose you've been working here long enough?' he asked.

'Two month yon scaffold's been up,' the man answered promptly, 'and I doubt if the work 'll be done afore winter. That's twenty families have had to seek new homes, for they had to turn out, ye ken, afore we could start.'

'Yes, of course.' Pat looked up at the blind broken windows peering between the three wooden platforms. 'Nobody could possibly live in the place with all this going on.'

'Ye'd be surprised how many o' them wanted to try it,' the men replied, 'but then, some folks get real attached to their ain corner. We had to get a sheriff's officer to some o' them afore they would move.'

They went back through the little door into the street. 'There you are,' Pat told Will triumphantly. 'I'm bound to know my own sister better than you, aren't I?'

Will said he guessed Pat was right, and he was real shocked at Janet for telling such stories. Little girls in the States, he added, were taught the difference between truth and falsehood when they were half Janet's age. Then he noticed, at first with relief, that Janet had stopped crying. But she was in a towering rage, which was worse.

'I *told* you the truth!' she screamed. 'Every bit of it! I saw the old man and he showed me the yellow box and how to make the little bird sing. And I slipped on the fish-scales, so there!'

They led her hastily towards the tram.

Chapter VIII

THE HOUSE OF THE PELICAN

PAT sat beside Mr Bloomfield in the big hired Bentley as they nosed their way out of the city and into the countryside. The rolling fields had been reaped of their oats and barley, and spread, undulating, towards the horizon. Sometimes the crest of a hill would be topped by huge granaries and outbuildings, with the farmhouse standing a little way off, approached by a tree-bordered lane. To Pat's English eyes the houses looked rather bleak and staring, but Mrs Bloomfield thought them very quaint because they were made of stone.

'All the same,' said Mr Bloomfield, ' those patchwork fields make me feel cramped. I'm not very partial to fences.'

'How else could you keep the cattle out of them?' Pat inquired.

'We raise our grain in one part of the country and our cattle in another,' said Mr Bloomfield, grinning.

Mrs Bloomfield sat wondering if they would encounter Lord Drumfingal himself. She had a great respect for the British aristocracy, and had met one or two members of it over in the States. But she wanted to see one on his own ground, and she very much hoped that he would appear.

They passed through the village of Drumfingal, with its grey one-storeyed houses capped by red tiles. Pat rather missed the warm timbering of the English cottages he had glimpsed on his travels with his father. The Scots ones had a rose-bush or two growing in front of them, and a well-kept vegetable patch at the back, but he missed the riot of colour permitted by the softer English landscape.

'There's an awful lot of stone about Scotland,' he said.

'From what I've seen of it,' answered Mr Bloomfield, 'you've got to be real tough to live here. That's why the people have made such a mark when they get out of it. They can survive anything. As for stone, well, I guess Edinburgh's a sort of monument to what can be done with a mason's chisel. It's one of the most beautiful cities I've seen.'

'Look!' Mrs Bloomfield suddenly pointed. 'Isn't that Drumfingal Castle?'

A little wood hid most of it except the old tower. A pair of white gates now appeared, letting in to a drive which wandered through the wood. Another car was passing up the drive before them, and a bus-load of sight-seers were buying tickets of admission at the lodge just beside the gates. Mr Bloomfield stopped his car and bought some tickets too. Then they went on up the drive, and presently came into sight of the castle.

The front of it was covered with yellow plaster, and had a flight of steps leading up to a hooded porch with a group of pillars on each side. Mrs Bloomfield had seen houses something like this in the States, where the rich people of colonial times had built their mansion houses in the same style in the eighteenth century. But behind this elegant façade there peered the remnants of the much older fortress-castle with its tower and turrets still standing. Pat and Will fixed their eyes on it as they left the car. That was the part they were interested in, however much the front portion had been decorated by this Robert Adam or whoever he was. . . .

But Mrs Bloomfield insisted upon examining the Adam rooms first, since that was what she had come for. The boys wandered rather wearily after her, staring up at the delicate green or blue ceilings with their sugar-icing decorations, while Mr Bloomfield looked appreciatively at the brocaded sofas and chairs and guessed that they didn't make such fabrics nowadays.

A number of other people trailed through the rooms, too, and Mrs Bloomfield examined each of them sharply. But none of the men looked as though the place belonged to him, and there was no sign anywhere of Lord Drumfingal. So presently she suggested that Pat might like some tea, and they could order ice-cream if any was to be had. And they sat down thankfully in the little cream-and-gold ballroom, now full of small tables and waitresses hurrying about with cups of tea.

'I don't know what you think, Ambrose,' Mrs Bloomfield said to her husband, 'but it strikes me as perfectly tragic that a beautiful ballroom like this should be filled with people like us.'

Mr Bloomfield pointed out very reasonably that if it wasn't filled with people like them, all paying a good price for their tea and the privilege of looking around them, it might not be kept up at all.

'Well, you know what I mean,' she replied; 'all the little tables should be cleared away, and there should be a small string band playing up in that gallery, and we should be wearing brocades, not tweeds, to be in keeping.'

'I don't know if I'd care about walking around in brocade,' said Mr Bloomfield, while the boys sniggered involuntarily. 'Now, does anyone want more so-called ice-cream? No? Well, I'm not surprised. This stuff tastes just like frozen flannel. If you've seen everything you want to, we might as well be getting back to the car.'

The only thing Mrs Bloomfield still wanted to see was Lord Drumfingal, but apparently he was invisible. She was just about to agree to their leaving when, much to her and her husband's surprise, the boys who had shown little interest in the place, now looked disappointed.

'There's that old bit at the back,' Will pointed out; 'it looks interesting, and there might be a dungeon or two. Can't we just have a look at it while we're here?'

At first they were not sure if it was shown to the public, but a notice just outside the ball-room said, 'To the Tower.' So they went down a long passage, up a crooked stone stairway and presently entered a room much grimmer and barer than the ones they had left behind.

It was about two hundred years older as well, and Mrs Bloomfield was not enthusiastic as she looked around at the narrow windows let in at a depth of several feet in the thickness of the walls. There was nothing in the room either, except an old oak table in the middle of it, and some dark, not very good portraits around the walls. The period which the room represented did not hold any interest for Mrs Bloomfield, who considered the Middle Ages very uncultured. Still, there was a bit in the guide-book about the tower and its contents. She found the place and began to read some parts aloud :

> . . . remnant of the ancient home of the Barons Drumfingal. In the upper hall of the Tower is to be found a selection of family portraits including one, by an unknown artist, of the ill-fated Lady Eglantine Drumfingal who, for daring to attend the Ball at Holyrood Palace in honour of the Young Pretender against her husband's wishes, was kept in close confinement by him in one room of his house on the Royal Mile, until death released her.

'Husbands surely had privileges in those days,' Mr Bloomfield commented, walking towards the picture. The boys drifted over as well, their curiosity awakened by the thought of someone's being imprisoned just for attending a ball. The portrait showed a rather white-faced woman with slanting eyes and a bodice festooned with lace. Her hair was scraped back from her forehead and powdered, and one hand with long tapering fingers touched a rose at her breast.

The painting was not very good, and the eyes looked beady and expressionless. Mrs Bloomfield examined Lady Eglantine's dress very carefully. It was an elaborate one, and she wondered aloud whether perhaps it was the very ball-dress in which she had appeared before the Young Pretender ?

'What's a Young Pretender anyway,' Will muttered, rather tired of the story by now.

'Why Willington, I'm surprised at you ! You know perfectly well he was Prince Charles Edward Stuart, the last of the Stuarts, and he came back and took Edinburgh, and gave a great ball in that very room you saw yesterday in the Palace ! I suppose Lady Eglantine's husband must have been a Jacobite and that was what made him so mad.'

'She looks perfectly wooden, like a doll.'

Mr Bloomfield pointed out, 'You'd probably look a bit wooden yourself after being shut up for—I wonder how long she was imprisoned before she died ?'

'Twelve and a half years.'

They all spun round at the sound of the deep voice behind them. An old man had come into the room without their noticing, and had been standing quietly listening to their conversation. He must have been very tall and powerful when he was young, but now he was rather bent, and his tweeds hung loosely on him.

'I agree with you about my ancestress's appearance, young man,' he addressed Will. 'But perhaps the artist is rather to blame for that. As for her pallor, well, twelve and a half years' confinement in one room isn't good for the complexion. Though I think, myself, that the colours have just faded.'

Mrs Bloomfield grasped first who he was. 'Are you Lord Drumfingal ?' she asked.

'I am. You, I think, are Americans ? A great many Americans come to see my house every year. And they all seem to find Lady Eglantine's history most absorbing.'

Mr Bloomfield cleared his throat. 'If you will forgive

my saying it, sir, the unfortunate lady seems to have been punished beyond her deserts.'

Lord Drumfingal went up to the picture-frame and tapped one corner of it. 'Wood-worm,' he muttered absently; 'I must let the National Trust authorities know. It's up to them now, thank heaven.' He turned politely to the man at his elbow. 'I beg your pardon. You were saying something?'

'I can't help thinking that twelve years' house confinement was rather a sharp reprisal for disobeying orders. If I may say so, her husband seems to have magnified her offence considerably.'

'He had very good reasons for keeping her under close observation. You will not find the whole story in that Guide. My ancestor was strongly against the return of the Stuarts. His wife was as strongly for it. He learned that she was in constant communication with the Jacobites and, in fact, acted as a spy for them here in Edinburgh——'

'H'm. So the lady was a spy, was she?' Mr Bloomfield moved towards the picture again. It was almost impossible to imagine that pale shadow of a woman doing anything so exciting.

'Yes. He intercepted a letter from her to the Young Pretender's father in France. It gave the disposition of the Government troops in the Castle. To prevent her from gathering and sending on any more information he kept her a virtual prisoner in the House of the Pelican——'

'The House of the Pelican!' The two boys stared at each other excitedly.

Lord Drumfingal seemed a little put out by the interruption. 'Rather a strange name, certainly, but it derives from our family crest, a pelican. One was carved above the old town house of the family on the Royal Mile. It was quite a common fashion in these days to emblazon one's residence with some such family symbol——'

'Whereabouts is the house?' Will interrupted eagerly. 'I—I'd give quite a lot to see it.'

'Don't interrupt, Willington,' his mother was saying, but Lord Drumfingal looked quite amiable again, and was obviously pleased by Will's enthusiasm.

'It seems strange, but I really don't know. As soon as Lady Eglantine's son succeeded he sold the old house at once, not caring to possess anything connected with his mother's long ordeal. About that time there was a great migration to the New Town, with its more salubrious air. The Royal Mile became a decayed slum, and later on many of the old houses were taken down. I always understood that the House of the Pelican was one of them.'

'Excuse me, but are you quite certain?'

'It isn't mentioned in the guide-book,' Mrs Bloomfield interrupted hastily, afraid lest her son should seem rude. 'And I'm sure, Willington, that Lord Drumfingal should know, if anyone does.'

'I feel quite flattered by the young man's interest in my ancestress,' Lord Drumfingal said kindly, 'but I fear that I cannot satisfy it. Lady Eglantine's immediate descendants had, naturally, a perfect horror of the place. They got rid of it as quickly as possible and never went near it again. Yes, I am really afraid that it must have been taken down long ago.'

Mrs Bloomfield, having attained her two objects in seeing the Adam decorations and Lord Drumfingal, said she thought they had occupied enough of his time and had better be going. The car had been parked a little way down the drive, so they had to walk down to it, Mr and Mrs Bloomfield going first and the boys lagging behind.

'Of all the queer things!' Will exclaimed. 'I wonder if Janet's tale could possibly be true?'

'I'm afraid, knowing Janet, it was probably just a coincidence,' Pat replied. 'Though it *is* queer, I grant you. But pelicans are quite usual animals on crests—I've seen one carved on a tombstone in an old church. And I still believe that Janet had seen the other stone carvings above the doorways down the Royal Mile, and remembered the pelicans in the Zoo and put the two things together.'

'The House of the Pelican!' Will muttered softly. 'It's a fine name anyway. I don't believe the civic authorities would let a name like that die out, if the house still existed. They've got everything named and labelled all over Edinburgh because of the tourist trade. If they didn't use *that* label, then I'm just afraid the old boy must be right. The house isn't there any longer.'

They were now approaching the gates, which they had not noticed particularly when driving through because they had been in such a hurry to see the house. The gateposts were quite imposing, being two pillars of stone with large balls on top, and a bird carved out of stone standing on each of them. The sun was now declining a little behind the pillars, and the birds with their heavy beaks stood up black against the sky.

'Pelicans. I wonder we didn't notice them.' Pat hurried forward as he spoke, hoping that he might be allowed to have a look at the Guide. But Mrs Bloomfield held it firmly in her hands as usual, and said she would read them all the historical bits they had missed while they drove home.

Her voice boomed steadily through the car as they drove along. When she had finished everything about Drumfingal, her son, rather to her surprise, asked her to read some more. He asked her if there was a list of old houses along the Royal Mile, and there was. He then asked her if she would read their names out.

Delighted that Willington was taking such an interest in the past, she did so. Boswell's Close, Sempill's Close, Gladstone's Land, Bell's Wynd, Fountain Close, Morocco Land—the old names sounded above the hum of the car. But in all that long list there was no mention whatever of the once-famous House of the Pelican.

Chapter IX

THE MYSTERY OF MR AND MRS BOND

MR and Mrs Bond always seemed to eat their lunch in a great hurry. Generally they missed out pudding altogether, pushing back their chairs and asking Mrs Mac-Kendrick to excuse them because they liked to start their afternoons early. The other guests would hear the front door closing a few minutes afterwards, and anyone sitting near the window could see them hurrying up the Square on their short, fat legs as if fearful of missing the tram at the corner of it.

Mr and Mrs Bond had become quite a puzzle to the other guests in Mrs MacKendrick's boarding-house. They seemed quite amiable and chatty, and yet in the end they told very little about themselves. They did not appear to have any settled home, but to wander about from town to town. Even Mr Foley, who had wakened up from his rather quiet sad manner when he found they knew so many foreign capitals with which he was also acquainted, could not make out what they had been doing there. For it appeared that they never had any time for ordinary sight-seeing.

Not even in Edinburgh. Of course everyone thought, at first, that their hurry to get out each afternoon was on account of the many excursions which started at two o'clock. But though no-one liked to ask directly what they had been doing with themselves, it appeared that they had not even found time to visit the Castle, let alone climb to the top of the Scott Monument.

'Well, I suppose we must do that next, mustn't we, Mother?' Mr Bond would say, when Chris asked if they had seen Holyrood Palace or been down the Royal Mile. She began to wonder if they went to the Zoo every afternoon to watch the sea-lions. But if they did, there would have been no need for so much hurry. They could have taken their time, and their pudding too, and still have had as much of the Zoo as they liked. . . .

And Janet was being difficult again. She had caught sight of a large poster showing a photograph of the beautiful lady in the train, and was clamouring to be taken to the theatre to see her. Her father told her she would not understand a word of the play, since it was all in French, but that did not matter to Janet.

'I see there's a puppet theatre on at Heriot Hall.' Mrs MacKendrick tried to smooth oil on the troubled waters and distract Janet's attention. 'Now, yon's quite a nice entertainment to take a wee girl to. I'm sure you'd enjoy that far better.'

'What are puppets?' asked Janet.

'Well, I've never seen any myself, but it's a sort of Punch and Judy show.'

'I'm too old for them,' Janet said flatly.

'Just hand me over the paper, will you?' Mrs MacKendrick asked her daughter. She unfolded it on the table and cast her eye down the Entertainments Column. 'Here it is. Two-thirty at Heriot Hall. They're doing a fairy play, *Thumbelina* (that's the story about the girl that was just the size of a thimble, Janet), and then an acrobatic comedy, *Trixie the Trickster*. I'm sure it would be very amusing.'

Mr Foley pulled some money out of his pocket. He wanted a quiet afternoon, and suddenly saw a way of getting it. 'If Chris would be kind enough to take Janet, I'll stand the tickets,' he said.

They held their breath, waiting for Janet's reactions. Fortunately the second title on the programme rather caught her fancy. '*Trixie the Trickster!*' she repeated thoughtfully. 'I wonder what it's about?'

'Best go and see.' Mr Foley pushed the money across the tablecloth towards Chris. 'It's sure to be much funnier than *Phèdre*,' he added persuasively.

Janet said that perhaps she could see the French play tomorrow instead, but she wouldn't mind going to *Trixie the Trickster* now. Greatly relieved at having stalled her for the time being, they all left the table, and Chris and Janet got on their things and started out.

Heriot Hall proved difficult to find. It was one of the little halls in the rather poorer part of the city, which small theatrical companies were in the habit of taking at Festival time, when they could not get anything better. Even

THE MYSTERY OF MR AND MRS BOND

Chris, who knew Edinburgh pretty thoroughly, had to ask once or twice before she could find the way. But presently they turned into a little street sprinkled with tobacconists' shops, ice-cream shops and fried-fish shops. And right at the end of it stood a plain stone building with two posters stuck one on each side of the door.

The posters were large and gaudy and hit one in the eye at some distance off. By this time a good many people were hurrying along the street, intent upon getting good seats to the front of the hall. Chris guessed that one would have to do the same in order to see such small things as puppets, so she only paused a moment to glance at the left-hand poster as they went in. It was adorned by a coloured drawing of a large sea-lion balancing a ball on its nose.

'Look!' Janet tugged at her hand. 'That's one of the things that barked at the Zoo!'

Chris was still staring, transfixed. For, under the titles of the two plays to be performed, was the name of the company giving them. It was called THE BOND PUPPET THEATRE, PROPRIETORS, MR AND MRS BOND.

'They can't be the same,' she told herself, buying two tickets mechanically from the little office just inside the door. 'They *said* they weren't Theatricals. . . .'

All the same, she hurried into the hall and looked eagerly about her. Of course there was no sign of the Bonds. There were a good many children present, and a sprinkling of grown-ups, but the stage was so tiny that at first she scarcely saw it at all. There it was, however, right down in front of her, a little gilded box set down on the edge of a platform, with red velvet curtains hanging down on each side of it.

Janet's face fell when Chris pointed it out to her. 'It's just a Punch and Judy show, like I said,' she complained; adding, 'I want to see the French lady in " Feedry". Isn't there time to go there instead?'

'H'sh!' Chris gave her a warning nudge. For the lights were dimming, and somebody had started playing a gramophone behind the red curtains. A row of bright little footlights sprang out suddenly before the small stage, and its own miniature curtain trembled, then drew aside to show a cottage with a rose-red tulip growing outside it. The tulip petals opened and Thumbelina jumped out of its heart to begin her story, from the time the huge toad hopped on to the stage and took her away, meaning to make her the wife of its horrible son.

Chris felt Janet stiffen with interest by her side. She herself felt rather superior to such a childish tale, but all the same she grew fascinated, watching it. The curious thing was that as the tale went on the stage seemed to grow larger, and the squeaky voices of the characters louder and more real. So did the music, which at first had sounded tinny and scraping. And presently both she and Janet seemed to be right inside the gilded frame, watching at close quarters while Thumbelina floated down the river (how did they make the river? With real water or pieces of glass? Chris found time to wonder), or begged for a grain of barley outside the home of the field-mouse.

Of course a lot of it had to do with the darkness inside the hall, which made the coloured lighting before them more real and vivid. For, as soon as Thumbelina's story was ended and the lights were put on again, the theatre shrank once more to the size of a box. All the children seemed to burst out talking together, and hardly quietened as the lights in the hall grew dim once more.

'Now for *Trixie the Trickster!*' Janet murmured.

The tiny curtain went up, and the footlights sparkled again. There stood Trixie, a whiskered sea-lion, revolving with dignity upon her rock and balancing a ball on the end of her nose. After she had tossed the ball up and down and caught it once or twice, she had some fun with her keeper, who was dressed in miniature uniform. She disdained the fish he had brought her, and brought out a huge fish herself from the depths of the pool. The fish did a dance too, looking so comic with its large goggle eyes that the smaller children in the audience squeaked with laughter. Finally, Trixie and the fish did a dance together, flipper to fin, and the curtain came down upon them still cavorting in front of the stage.

But Chris did not move towards the entrance along with the rest of the audience. She had seen a door by the side of one of the big red curtains, and she led Janet purposefully towards it. She was determined to find out if the Bonds were really the ones they knew.

On the other side of the door was a scene of great confusion. Somebody was lifting away the gramophone already, and somebody else was filling up a teapot from a kettle on a small stove. And there was Mrs Bond, looking rather more flushed than usual, pouring the milk into her cup first, as she always liked it at Mrs MacKendrick's.

When she saw them she gave her wide smile and said, 'Well, dearies! How did you like the show?'

'I laughed like anything,' Janet told her, 'and I'm glad after all that I didn't go and see "Feedry". Mr Bond did the sea-lion barking, didn't he? It sounded just like the one—the one I thought had got into the house one night.'

'I told him he shouldn't be practising it in the bedroom,' Mrs Bond said, 'but he wouldn't give over.'

Then they caught a glimpse of Mr Bond at the back of the stage. They saw the back of the toy theatre too, and there seemed to be a lot of wires stretched over its top. Mr Bond was in his shirt-sleeves and looked rather red and tired. He was taking the puppets off the wires. The big silver fish lay on the ground already, and he was trying to disentangle the sea-lion.

He waved one free hand towards them, calling to Janet, 'Like to come over and see how it works?'

Janet scrambled on to the platform at once, followed by Chris who was also curious. Mr Bond obligingly switched on the lights of the little theatre again, and they scrambled up on to another, smaller platform which allowed them to look down through the open top of the theatre. Trixie still hung on her wires, which were fixed to her tail, her flippers and her muzzle. Mr Bond obligingly pulled the wires and made her do a little dance. He also barked once or twice.

'So that's what you were doing at the Zoo!' Chris exclaimed.

Mr Bond nodded and began to haul Trixie up. 'I specialise in my animal turns,' he said. 'Lifelike, everyone calls 'em. Have you been in the Antwerp Zoo? No? Hours I've spent there. Hours.'

'Were you studying sea-lions there too?' Chris privately thought they must be the same everywhere, and he need not have gone so far afield.

'No, it was cockatoos that time. We were touring

the Continent, giving a novelty bird-ballet. The walk was easy enough; I got the hang of it in an hour. It was the screech I was studying. Hard on the throat.'

Chris looked at him rather reproachfully. 'I suppose this doesn't count as a real theatre,' she said, 'especially when you don't give evening performances, and don't come in late. But you did tell me you weren't Theatricals.'

Mr Bond took Trixie off the wires and gave her to Janet to hold. She was beautifully stuffed, and covered with real sealskin. Janet stroked her and listened to hear whether Mr Bond would confess to making up stories too.

But as soon as he had got his attention off the wires he burst out laughing instead. 'I'm very particular what I say. And what did I say? I said we weren't on the stage. That's right, isn't it? Trixie, she's on the stage. And Thumbelina, she's on it too. But not Mother and me. We're behind it, that's where *we* are!'

'That's right,' said Mrs Bond, taking a step or two nearer with the tea-cup still in her hand. 'We didn't intend to mislead you, but we were dead beat looking for rooms. And when your mother said she didn't take Theatricals, we thought, well, we'd better keep quiet about our profession, though it isn't the same thing at all.'

'Not in the least,' put in Mr Bond firmly.

Chris said hastily that all her mother was afraid of was people who needed early supper and something to eat when they arrived back late. Of course a tiny theatre like that wasn't like a real one, and they weren't any trouble at all in the house. Then they parted in a very friendly way, and Chris took Janet home again.

On the way there Janet said triumphantly, 'I *did* hear a sea-lion bark that night! I told you all, and nobody would believe me. Of course it was only Mr Bond practising in his room, but it sounded exactly like the one in the Zoo.'

'Well, maybe you did,' Chris conceded, 'but if it was only Mr Bond practising, then you certainly didn't see one looking through the skylight. Did you?'

Janet looked a little ashamed. 'No,' she said in a low voice, 'I made that bit up.'

'If you mix up true things and false things you might get into terrible trouble,' Chris told her severely; 'like the boy and the wolf.'

'What boy and wolf?' Janet looked interested.

'Well, there was a boy once, and he kept frightening people by calling out, "Wolf! Wolf!" and pretending he saw one. At first everybody rushed to help him with guns and axes and things. Then they saw he was only making up a story, so, when a real wolf came and chased him, and he called out, nobody came to help him and he was eaten up.'

'Oh!' said Janet, looking thoughtful.

'And that day you followed Effie'—Chris began warming to her work—'I dare say you did follow her, and then you lost sight of her, and began to play with those children instead. But you kept wondering where Effie had gone, so presently you made up that story in your own mind: all about the little wooden staircase and the old man and the yellow box——'

'I didn't make it up. I didn't!'

'Look here, Janet, Pat asked Effie if she'd been to a house with a stone pelican carved above it, and she didn't seem to know what he was talking about. So there!'

Janet looked astonished, and then a little uncertain.

'I'm *sure* I saw it,' she said after a minute, 'but—but sometimes I dream things or make them up in my mind, just to amuse myself. And then they become real.'

'Babies do that often.' Chris tried to speak kindly. 'And if they're the only ones in the family they sometimes make up brothers and sisters and really believe that they have them. I did that myself, but you've got to stop some time. And it's time you stopped now.'

Janet made no reply. But they were just stepping into the house now, and as she ran past Chris to take off her things Chris heard her mutter, 'There *was* a yellow box with a bird that sang. I saw it!'

By supper-time everyone knew about the Bonds and what they did with their afternoons, and everyone thought it very funny and interesting. Most of the guests determined to see the Bond Puppet Theatre for themselves, and even Mrs MacKendrick said she would take next Saturday afternoon off and visit the little theatre. They laughed, too, at Janet's sea-lion, and Mr Bond obligingly gave one or two barks at the supper table, just to let everyone know how well he could do it.

But Pat looked a little thoughtful. He was a fair-minded boy, and he did not like to remember all the rows he had given Janet for not speaking the truth. He even felt uneasily that perhaps he ought to apologise to her, though it was ridiculous to apologise to a child of nine. He was relieved when Chris came and told him that he was wanted on the telephone, because it stopped his thinking such thoughts.

The caller was Will Bloomfield. 'I've got to go to a concert with Mother tomorrow morning,' he began at once. 'Fancy starting music just after breakfast! But

Mother wants you and Janet to come to lunch afterwards at the hotel, if you can manage it. She remembers Janet in the train, and she wants to see her again.'

Pat sighed. Then he said, 'Yes, thank you, we can manage it. It's my turn to look after her anyway, because Chris took her to a puppet show this afternoon. And by the way, the people who run the theatre are staying here. Their name's Bond.'

'Why, that's interesting.' Will did not sound very interested all the same. 'Was the show good?'

'There was a comic scene with a performing sea-lion. Do you remember my telling you the fuss Janet made one night, insisting she heard a sea-lion bark? Well, she did. At least, she heard Mr Bond practising barking in his bedroom.'

'You don't say! And, there was a house with a pelican too, though we didn't believe it. Look, Pat, supposing the kid was telling the truth about that as well?'

'Oh, rats!' said Pat, and rang off.

Chapter X

ON THE TRAIL

ALL the same, he couldn't help wondering.

Not about the old man at the top of the staircase, of course, or the fish tails and the yellow box. They bore too clearly the hall-mark of Janet's vivid imagination. But there *had* been a house like that once. The House of the Pelican. Janet and he couldn't find it, and old Lord Drumfingal said it must have been taken down.

But supposing it hadn't?

Old Lord Drumfingal hadn't been very sure about that. And perhaps Janet had wandered farther afield with those children than she had thought. There was a whole stretch of the Royal Mile going down in the other direction, towards Holyrood Palace. No doubt there would be hoardings and repairs going on there too, and Janet had just got muddled. Anyway, he hadn't a thing to do tomorrow morning until lunch-time. He might just fill in the time by poking around a little. . . .

The sun had stopped shining today. It was even a little cold, and a queer grey mist had floated in from the waters of the Firth, away down at Leith. It seeped through the streets and lay like a long pale wave at the foot of the Castle Rock. Edinburgh people called it a 'haar', and in some queer way seemed rather proud of it. People from other places put on thicker coats and hurried a little as they walked.

The Royal Mile was even darker than usual, but that

made it more mysterious, as though it were hiding a secret at every step. Instead of beginning at the Castle end, this time Pat took a bus right down to the bottom of the long road, and getting out at the wrought-iron gates of Mary Stuart's little old palace, began to walk up again towards the Rock. It was an even poorer district at this end, and distinctly squalid. Children swarmed over the pavements; women came out of dark entries, banged rugs against the curb and vanished again; and the people went by like figures in a grey dream.

Pat had started out early, so as to penetrate through every gateway and step into every yard. It was slow going, as he wanted to examine both sides of the road, in case Janet had forgotten that she had crossed it earlier at one point. In that case the House of the Pelican would not even be on the same side of the street as the one at which she emerged. He asked a great many people who looked as if they belonged to the neighbourhood, and he inquired at the little shops along the route. All the people he asked spoke a much rougher and broader Scots than he had encountered so far, and it was difficult sometimes to make them out.

But when he did it was always to the same effect. Nobody had ever heard of a house of that name.

He had worked his way up to the top of the Mound again, and felt tired. Soon it would be time to go back

ON THE TRAIL

to Caroline Square and fetch Janet for the luncheon party at the hotel. More to give his legs a rest than because he was interested, he stopped to look in at a window full of old silver teapots and horn snuff-boxes, when someone already looking in at the window turned round sharply to hail him.

'Why, hullo! What are you doing up here again?'

It was Will. He explained that the concert had finished early, and he had parted from his mother, who had gone back to the hotel. 'I thought I'd just loaf around here a bit to kill time,' he explained, then corrected himself rather shamefacedly. 'At least, not to kill time exactly, but to have another look for that old house. Perhaps you and Janet missed it.'

Pat shook his head. 'I'm sure we didn't, not if it was where she said. But I thought she might have become muddled, so I've been hunting along the lower stretch. I've been into every courtyard and looked at every house between Holyrood Palace and this.'

'Well, I thought the same. Matter of fact, I'd meant to start from here and go downward, but there's hardly time, though Mother said half past one for lunch because she's got letters to write. Still, if you've looked....'

Pat wasn't listening. He was watching a figure get off the tram just at the corner and begin trudging up towards the Castle. They were standing just a few feet from the tram stop themselves, and the figure began to draw level with them. It was Effie the fishwife.

Pat took a step forward, meaning to greet her. Just then, however, a bunch of people came out of a shop and passed between them. When the people had passed Effie had passed as well, but now she had hastened her pace, and seemed bent on getting as far away from the boys as possible. Pat had a sudden strong feeling that she had seen him after all. Though, in that case, why should she not wish them to join her?

Yes, he was right. The shop window reflected her figure, and in it he saw her give a swift hurried look over her shoulder, and then stump on, faster than ever. On an impulse he turned towards Will, speaking abruptly:

'Don't look just now, but that was Effie who went past—you know, the fishwife that Janet said had led her to the house. If we follow her now she might lead us to it again.'

Will shrugged his shoulders good-naturedly, surprised at Pat's animation, but willing to do what he wanted. He could not imagine, if Pat had hunted properly before, that it was any use following a woman with a basket on her back. But then, he had not caught Effie's furtive look as she glanced back over her shoulder. . . .

'Don't let her see we're following her!' Pat breathed in his ear; 'and don't let her get out of sight either.'

They followed her blue apron as it moved up the street. She went quite confidently now, evidently thinking Pat had not seen her. Then she swerved to the left, disappearing down the very passage, by the side of the scaffolding, from which Janet had emerged.

'Careful now!' Pat warned as they approached it. Don't let's be too near the entry in case she sees us when she comes out.'

'Well, why shouldn't she?' Will protested at last. 'You said she didn't seem to know anything about the House of the Pelican. I guess she's just doing her usual round, though of course if it amuses you to follow her . . .'

Pat had strolled on, and now drew Will in with him to the doorway of a shop, from where he could keep an eye on the entry to the passage down which Effie had gone. 'I know it sounds crazy,' he said, 'but, after all, she didn't exactly say she had never heard of the house. She just more or less said she didn't know anything about pelicans. And she said it in a funny way too——'

'How do you mean, " a funny way "?'

'I didn't remember it until I saw she'd seen me down there at the corner and wanted to avoid me. She had a funny look on her face, and it was the same look she gave me when I asked about the house. As if she wanted to hide something——'

'Oh, all right! If you think she's really going on some sinister errand I don't mind waiting. But we mustn't be late for lunch.'

They waited. Presently Will looked at his watch. 'She must be doing a roaring trade in that courtyard. Or perhaps somebody hasn't got change. Are you sure she couldn't have slipped out again without our noticing?'

Pat was quite sure. His eyes had been glued to the entry until now they felt glazed and tired. But the street was comparatively empty, since it was nearly lunch-time and most people had gone home for a meal. It would have been impossible to have missed Effie's picturesque figure once it had showed itself on the pavement again.

Will shivered slightly, moving from one foot to the other. The haar still crept up the street, touching everyone with its damp breath. He felt hungry too, and looked at his watch again.

'We've been standing here for a good half-hour. Maybe she's fallen down in a fit. What about going to see?'

Pat was cold too, and tired of waiting. 'We can't stand here all day,' he conceded, 'so perhaps we'd better.'

It was the same courtyard in which they had found Janet playing with the other children. What looked like the same washing hung out on ropes above their heads. The same stone buildings stood tightly, shoulder to shoulder, about the yard with only a narrow passage leading between them farther back from the street. And there was no sign of Effie anywhere.

'There you are!' said Will. 'I expect she's gone into one of the houses to have her own dinner. Maybe some friends of hers live here.'

Some of the doors were private entrances, a few even bearing dusty unpolished brass plates. The flats in each house were piled one on top of each other and were reached by a dark corkscrew stone stairway, which gaped at them from the bottom of the tallest building of all. It must have been a perfect rabbit-warren of a place, judging from the clatter and voices which came out of the row upon row of windows stretching upward, and floated down to the two boys outside.

'She might be anywhere,' Will said, turning away.

Just then a shapeless sort of woman without a hat and

clutching a shopping bag, came out into the court. Instinctively Pat stopped her. 'Excuse me,' he said, 'but has Effie the fishwife been at your door?'

'Aye,' said the woman, 'but if it's fish ye're wantin', ye canna get her noo. She's awa' back oot.'

'Back oot?' Pat was so surprised he copied the woman's speech. 'Where?'

'Oot-by,' said the woman, hurrying past them out of the court.

'It seems to me,' remarked Will, 'that there is some subtle difference between " oot " and " oot-by ", but I'm hanged if I know what it is. D'you think they publish a dictionary of the local language?'

'We must have missed her after all!' Pat felt bewildered. 'Though I'm sure I never took my eyes off that doorway. . . .'

They went back into the street, past the Outlook Tower on the one side and the big hoardings on the other. They were hurrying now, because it was almost one o'clock. This end of the street was livelier than the other, and a number of people were also hurrying in front of them towards the tram stop.

Pat stopped suddenly on the pavement, clutching Will's arm. 'Look!' he exclaimed. 'If that isn't Effie, it's awfully like her!'

The big fishwife in the blue skirt had reached the tram stop and was boarding a tram. She had slipped the strap of the creel from her head, and she turned towards the conductor as he took the basket from her and stowed it away. They saw her side-face quite clearly. It *was* Effie.

The next moment the tram had gone.

'Now, how on earth did she manage that?' said Pat, staring.

'Why, she must have been walking down the street in front of us all the while. We just never noticed.'

'Then where did she come from? I'll swear she never came out of that courtyard! Not just in front of us anyway, or we'd have seen her at once. But she must have come from somewhere just a few minutes ahead of us. She wasn't any distance off.'

Will looked puzzled. Then his face cleared. 'I know what she did! She *must* have come out of that passage when you weren't looking. Then she walked *up* the hill, towards the Castle you know, when we were talking and didn't notice her pass. Then she came *down* again while we were in that yard at the end of the passage. She probably passed by the mouth of it while we were talking to that woman and had our backs turned . . . .'

To Pat's mind, there were too many 'ifs' and 'probablys'. He didn't want to risk another disagreement with Will, but he was perfectly certain in his own mind that, while they stood in the entrance to the shop, he had not let a single person pass by, or emerge farther down, without scrutiny. No, there was something strange about the whole business of Effie's appearances and disappearances.

Their own tram appeared, and they ran forward to catch it. Behind them the one o'clock gun suddenly boomed out, its echoes following them down the tall and shadowy street, shaking the old windows a little, eddying, muffled, into the forgotten courts lying behind the houses; momentarily disturbing the air which still seemed to hang heavy with the secrets of centuries past.

Chapter XI

THE LITTLE GOLD BOX

'No, not lobster, dear. It's bad for little girls.' Mrs Bloomfield spoke kindly but firmly to Janet, and her husband declined the head waiter's offer with a sigh, so as to set a good example. He was very fond of lobster.

Janet was on her best behaviour and made no demur. She was given chicken instead, and picked at it daintily, while Mrs Bloomfield turned to converse with Pat. 'My husband is so looking forward to hearing the Farewell Symphony ! And your father is privileged to be playing in it, I hear. Imagine helping to put a masterpiece before the world for the first time !'

'He's not got a solo part,' Pat said quickly ; 'he's just playing among the trombones.'

'Ah, yes. Toscani's your first trombone.' Mr Bloomfield was joining in the conversation more than usual, because it was the sort that he liked. 'Extraordinary what effects Strauss could get with the brass sections,' he went on ; adding regretfully, 'our own orchestra at Fairport is weak on brass.'

'Still, you've found one or two players for it already,' Mrs Bloomfield reminded him. 'That's what he's here for,' she told the others, 'and I guess he hasn't missed a single orchestral concert since we've come.'

'Well,' said Mr Bloomfield, 'I happen to be one of the largest guarantors of our orchestra back home, and I know a bit about music too. Of course, all I can do is to make recommendations to our committee, but most of my recommendations go through.'

'I suppose yours is a permanent orchestra?' Pat asked rather wistfully. 'I mean, it doesn't have to travel about all over the place?'

'Why, of course not ! We have a summer season as well as a winter one, and the members just live in Fairport and own the dearest little homes !' Mrs Bloomfield was just as enthusiastic as her husband. 'The people of Fairport are very cultured,' she said.

'I think I would like to live in a dear little home in America !' Janet said in a dreamy voice. 'I wish Mr Toscani was dead.'

'Why, Janet !' Mrs Bloomfield looked shocked. 'What a thing to say ! Don't you like Mr Toscani?'

'Yes, he's all right. But if he was dead he couldn't play the solo trombone part—Father would play it. Father plays just as well as he does, but Mr Toscani got into the orchestra first. And if Father played it, and Mr Bloomfield was listening——'

'Shut up, Janet!' her brother interrupted in a hurry; 'and finish your chicken or you'll not come to the ice-cream.'

He felt very embarrassed, and all three Bloomfields began talking at once, so as to cover the awkward moment. Fortunately Janet's attention was deflected by the need for choosing between a pink ice-cream and a Neapolitan one. When they had finished the excellent lunch, it became clear that the Bloomfields intended the Foleys to spend the afternoon with them too.

'Now, where's my list?' Mrs Bloomfield produced one, with the items checked off. 'I tried to plan for an exhibition that would interest Janet. Has she been taken to any of the exhibitions yet? No? Well, I always think you can't interest a child in historical subjects too early. Now, there's a very, very interesting collection of old toys and musical boxes on loan from various Scots families. I just thought that might be a good thing to visit this afternoon, seeing my husband collects musical boxes anyway.'

'You've got the biggest collection of them in Massachusetts, haven't you, Father?' Will said rather proudly.

'Why, not the biggest, but maybe the finest. I'm not a millionaire you know.'

'If you'd only remember that, Ambrose, I'd be gratified. You spend far too much on those artificial little tinkling things, when real living music——'

Mr Bloomfield called the waiter over and paid the bill. Pat had enjoyed his lunch, and he knew he would enjoy the luxury of driving in the Bloomfields' expensive car. Out of gratitude for those two things, he was prepared to suffer the waste of time spent on such things as old toys and musical boxes.

By now, as so often happened in Edinburgh, the sun had come out and the haar had dispersed as by magic. They drove to the exhibition which was in a beautiful old house just behind Princes Street, and found the objects displayed in two large rooms with polished oak floors. At first Pat and Will felt cheered, supposing that they could walk round the two rooms quickly and out again.

But this time it was Mr Bloomfield who lingered. He lingered over each separate musical box, from the oblong ones with brass rolls inside them which revolved so that their tiny prongs caught on a sort of comb, to the elaborate groups of dancing figures set in motion by the turn of a key.

Presently he came to a stop before a glass case full of little musical boxes so precious that they were locked away from the public. 'Now these are really valuable,' he told Pat, pointing to a velvet-lined shelf upon which lay one or two elaborately enamelled snuff-boxes which played a tune when you took off the lid. 'Especially that one.' He pointed to the one just below the snuff-boxes, placed on a shelf all by itself.

It was a little gold box with a golden bird on the lid. 'It doesn't play tunes,' Mr Bloomfield explained, 'but when you touch the spring, the bird sings and, believe me, it sings the true nightingale note. I've seen two such, one in New York and one in a museum in Paris. They're very rare. I've been looking for one myself, for years.'

'Then I hope you won't find it. It's sure to cost a fortune,' his wife said.

'Now then Hannah. Whatever you say, my dear, I'd

THE LITTLE GOLD BOX

give a thousand dollars for a box like that ; yes, and five hundred to anyone who can lead me to it. But I wish they hadn't locked up the case. I'd surely like to hear that bird sing.'

Mrs Bloomfield had put on her glasses and was reading the label beneath the box. ' Who do you think it belongs to ? It's on loan from Lord Drumfingal ! You remember, Ambrose ? That nice old gentleman who showed us his pictures the other day ! '

' Lord Drumfingal ! ' Mr Bloomfield looked thoughtful. ' Now I wonder——'

' You surely can't insult him by asking him if he would sell it ? '

' Maybe he wouldn't consider an offer of a thousand dollars in the light of an insult. Anyway, there he is, over there. I'm going to ask him.'

The tall old man going quietly round the room had had his back to them up to now, but Mr Bloomfield had caught a glimpse of his face in a mirror, and went up to him at once. But though he put his suggestion as tactfully as possible, it was obvious that Lord Drumfingal could not be persuaded to sell.

So Mr Bloomfield dropped the matter with a face of great disappointment. ' At any rate, sir, could you allow me the privilege of hearing the bird-note ? This case seems locked, but possibly you could persuade somebody to produce the key.'

A listening attendant was just going to say no, when one look from the haughty old gentleman extinguished him. ' Kindly fetch the curator,' Lord Drumfingal said, ' and tell him to bring the key of this case. I am the owner of that box, and I wish to show it to my friends.'

THE HOUSE OF THE PELICAN

The curator arrived with the key on hearing who wanted it; but he stayed with them so as to guard the other exhibits, as it was really against regulations to open the showcase at all. Lord Drumfingal picked up the little box and held it in his hands for a moment or two.

'It has been in my family for nearly two hundred years,' he said, looking at it lovingly, 'and when I was a little boy I was given it to play with on Sundays. I don't really believe I have heard it since. I only hope I can remember how it works.'

The box was elaborately carved. He pressed the little leaves and flowers on it here and there, but nothing happened. He frowned. 'There's a small spring, and one only has to touch it for the bird to open its beak and sing. Dear me! How very tiresome if I can't find the spring!'

Mr Bloomfield asked to be allowed to try. He said he had known several boxes with secret springs, and he was sure he could find this one. But he didn't. Then the curator asked Lord Drumfingal how long it was, exactly, since he had actually heard the bird sing. Lord Drumfingal stood still a moment, calculating.

'Not since I was a boy,' he repeated, 'and that's—dear me, I'm afraid that is quite sixty years ago. Since then it has stayed in a cabinet at Drumfingal.'

The curator shook his head sadly. 'I'm afraid, your Lordship, that the mechanism will have got rusty. And I really don't know of anyone who can repair such things nowadays.'

Janet had become tired of examining the little dancing figures round a maypole at the other end of the room. She hadn't bothered to join them when they opened the case, for a glance towards it had shown her that it contained no dolls. But now she took a few steps toward them and saw clearly, for the first time, what they were looking at.

'It's another little yellow box!' she exclaimed.

Pat started; but Janet was looking now at the bird on the lid.

'And it sings. Why don't you make it sing?'

'Well, we've all been trying to,' said Lord Drumfingal, 'but we can't find the spring. I knew where it was once, but I've forgotten.'

'You just press the little knob under the bird's tail,' Janet told him quite casually; adding, 'if you hold the box sideways you'll see it.'

Lord Drumfingal held the box sideways. The drooping paradise-tail of the bird had quite hidden that portion of the box, but now that the light struck through the small space between the delicately carved feathers and the lid he could see, sticking up, a tiny gold knob no bigger than the head of a pin.

'Ah ! I remember now !' he exclaimed, and managed to touch it with his little finger. There was a click and whirr inside the box, which seemed to vibrate slightly between his hands. The bird opened its golden beak, and a pure true nightingale trill echoed through the room.

Mr Bloomfield turned sharply towards Janet. 'Now, how in creation did you know that ?'

'Because that's how the old man made the other box play. It was exactly like this one.'

'Do you mean you know where another box is, like this one ?'

Janet gave a defiant glance towards her brother and nodded her head. 'I told Pat about it, but he thought I was making it up. It belongs to an old man who lives up a little wooden staircase, where Effie the fishwife went. He let me play with it, and he showed me the knob.'

They stared at each other, and then at her. Then Mr Bloomfield said excitedly, 'Where does this old man live, Janet ? I'd sure like to buy that box !'

'I don't know,' said Janet. 'Pat and I tried to find the house again, but we couldn't. That's why he couldn't believe me.'

Mr Bloomfield still looked excited..

'I've been hunting clear over Europe for another box like that !' he almost shouted. 'And what's more, I'd give one thousand dollars for one. Gladly. And five hundred to whichever of you can find the place where it is ! That's not a reward, if you don't like taking rewards ; it's payment for a commissioned job of work.'

THE LITTLE GOLD BOX

There was a silence. Even Mrs Bloomfield did not say anything. Perhaps she was too appalled at the thought of all those dollars.

Then Pat gave a sigh. 'I've looked for the house twice. It's somewhere down on the Royal Mile—at least, it's there if it's anywhere ; but nobody's even heard of a house with a pelican carved on the door——'

'Oh, the House of the Pelican?' Lord Drumfingal looked as if he had suddenly seen a light. 'I told you it must have been taken down years ago. I've never even seen the place myself!'

'Well, this fishwife—what d'you call her?—Effie. Janet said she'd seen her there. If you know who she is, can't you ask her?'

'I did ask her, sir. She doesn't seem to know anything about it either. But I think . . .' Pat hesitated.

'Well, come on, boy! What do you think?'

'I think she's only pretending she doesn't know. Though I can't imagine why.'

The little bird had stopped singing. The box gave another click and was silent. Lord Drumfingal handed it back to the curator, who put it on to its shelf again and locked up the case. They all stared thoughtfully at Janet. Pat began to speak in rather a garbled way, put out by the steady stare with which Janet was regarding him.

'I've spent two whole mornings hunting for that house, just to see if Janet was speaking the truth or not. She generally means to, but she gets things mixed up in her mind. Perhaps she saw a musical box like that one in a shop, and was even shown how it played ; and then she wandered about the Royal Mile and saw some old house with a wooden staircase, and thought that was a more romantic place to find the box in. . . .' His voice died away into silence.

'The box belonged to the old man up the staircase,' Janet said obstinately, 'and there were bits of old fish lying all around and an awful smell.'

'That's the sort of thing she says,' Pat told them helplessly; 'and as for the pelican, well, we were looking at them in the Zoo.'

'Pelicans or no pelicans, my offer holds good,' Mr Bloomfield announced. 'One thousand dollars to the owner of a box like that one, and five hundred to anyone who leads me to it. Payment for an honest job of work.'

Chapter XII

A CAT AND A CLUE

'FIVE hundred dollars!' Chris exclaimed.
'It's about two hundred pounds. But what's the use? We can't find the house, or the old man either.'

Pat and Chris were talking the whole thing over in the empty drawing-room of Number Seven. It was the half-hour before the evening meal, when all the others had gone to their rooms to tidy, or to make ready for going out to a theatre or concert afterwards. Chris had heard all about Janet's adventure up on the Royal Mile just after it happened. She had heard Pat scolding Janet for making things up; but she had heard, too, about their visit to Drumfingal Castle, and how Lord Drumfingal had told them about the House of the Pelican.

She had little time to do more than listen to what other people told her. Even Mrs MacKendrick was sorry for Chris. But what could she do? She had to ask Chris to stay in and help her with the housework, now they were so busy. All she could manage was to promise her daughter a nice treat when the Festival was over.

When the Festival was over!—Chris sighed. It was a bit hard to see Pat going out every day and having a nice time with those rich Bloomfields. She hadn't grudged the older guests going out and amusing themselves, because people had funny ideas of amusement once they were grown-up; but Pat would probably have liked doing the same things as herself. . . .

The rather bleak look on her face made him remember something. 'Janet was talking about you to Mrs Bloomfield,' he said rather awkwardly, 'and the Bloomfields asked if you ever got out to enjoy yourself. They said if your mother could spare you tomorrow afternoon, they'd like to take you out with them somewhere.'

'In the big Bentley?' Her face lit up. 'I'd love to come, and I'm sure Mother will say it's all right.'

Mrs MacKendrick not only said it was all right, she took pity on both Chris and Pat and promised to look after Janet while they were out. Mr Foley was busier than ever with the New English Orchestra, which was playing the new Strauss work next week. All the big critics, and most of the other visiting musicians who were not playing themselves that night, were going to be there. The symphony was a very difficult one and needed a great deal of rehearsal. Mr Foley grew thinner and quieter than ever under the strain, and less and less able to devote any time to Janet.

Chris was very thoughtful that evening, everyone noticed. She seemed to have something worrying her. She was absent-minded about handing things at table, and didn't seem to hear what anyone said. Later in the evening, when she was helping her mother with the visitors' beds, she said suddenly, 'Mother, how much would it cost to get a new mattress for every room?'

'A good deal. Mind and not crumple the bedspread, dearie.'

'Would two hundred pounds be enough?'

'I should think so. But where would we get two hundred pounds?'

Chris was holding the bedspread in her teeth to assist

A CAT AND A CLUE

in getting it into the right folds. When she managed to speak again she said, 'Once the beds are comfortable we can put up our prices to the same as other people's. I don't see the fun of working as hard as we do unless we can make a profit.'

Mrs MacKendrick sighed. 'Anything we make over the Festival will have to go to repaper the hall. The wallpaper's terrible and so's the paint. And the hall's the first thing people see. A shabby hall puts them off at the start.'

Chris relapsed into silence again. Her mother glanced oddly at her once or twice, but received no information about what was in the girl's mind.

Pat was to take her to the North Caledonian Hotel at two o'clock the next afternoon. It would be a rush, dressing and reaching it in time, but Mrs MacKendrick told Chris not to bother about the washing-up, as she would do it herself. Chris swallowed her lunch quickly next day, so as to have as long a time as possible to titivate. Apart from the outing, she was excited by the thought of meeting Pat's friends. Americans never came to a place like Mrs MacKendrick's guest house, so she had met very few; but from what Pat had said, she liked the sound of them, and she didn't want to disgrace him by her appearance either.

She brushed her fair reddish hair till it shone, wishing heartily that it was either longer or shorter. If it had been shorter, she could have done it in a page-boy bob, and if longer, well, there were all sorts of interesting and unusual things that she might have done with it then. As it was, she could only make it into the usual horse-tail with a new ribbon, very tightly bound.

Hat? Nothing but her school felt, as she didn't

generally wear one, so no hat. Her new coat, though it was extremely hot, and would no doubt feel like a blanket before the end of the afternoon. Gloves? She looked at her nails, which were badly shaped and rather bitten. Gloves were a frightful nuisance and she hardly ever wore them, but perhaps it might be as well. . . .

Then she suddenly remembered her mother's nail varnish. It was a new bottle which Mrs MacKendrick had bought to decorate herself with for a friend's wedding. The varnish was a very bright pink, so she had only used it once, but Chris had rather admired the colour, holding that if you bothered to varnish your nails at all, people should notice the fact.

She left her room and went to the top of the stairs, listening. Voices still sounded from the dining-room, her mother's with them, so that was all right. Somehow Chris had a good idea that Mrs MacKendrick wouldn't allow her to colour her nails, so she didn't intend to ask. She slipped into her mother's room opposite, seized the little jar and began to blob the varnish on hurriedly, wishing she had done so before doing the rest of her dressing, because the instructions said you had to let the varnish dry, and not let anything touch it.

Somebody opened the dining-room door. 'Are you ready, Chris?' Pat called up the stairs.

'Just coming!' She ran out of the room and downstairs, keeping her fingers carefully stretched out and not touching her coat. Pat opened the hall door and they ran down the steps and along the Square.

'I smell bananas!' Pat sniffed as he ran; 'and why are you holding your hands like that?'

'It's nail varnish, and it's got to dry.'

A CAT AND A CLUE

He glanced down at her fingers. 'What a perfectly frightful colour! And just when we're going to meet the Bloomfields, too.'

Chris felt as if she could cry. 'I put it on specially for the Bloomfields, because they're your friends. It's *not* a frightful colour—it's called blush-rose. You don't think roses a frightful colour, do you?'

He saw she was hurt, so tried hastily to make up for the unfortunate remark. 'Oh, I expect it's all right. I dare say Americans like that sort of thing. But can't you tuck your hands away or something? Surely they're dry by now!'

This cast rather a shadow over the expedition from the start, but the welcome the Bloomfields gave soon dispersed that. They were waiting in the central lounge of the hotel, and Mrs Bloomfield spoke very kindly to Chris, because she was sorry for any girl who had to make beds and wash dishes during the Festival instead of going out and getting some culture.

She was wearing gloves unfortunately, so Chris wasn't able to see what her nails were like; but the girl couldn't help feeling convinced, from the way Mrs Bloomfield dressed otherwise, that her nails wouldn't be painted at all. She dug her hands into the pocket of her coat, and tried to listen to what Mr Bloomfield was saying.

'Well, if we're all set, I'll just have the car brought round. There's an old ruin not far from here—Craigmillar Castle it's called—maybe we could have a look at it. Or what about the Forth Bridge? I'm told it's quite a triumph of engineering.'

Pat looked eager at the mention of the bridge, but Mrs Bloomfield, unfortunately, was not enthusiastic.

'That's Science,' she said, 'and I imagine we can do quite a lot in that way ourselves, so it seems a waste of time to cross the Atlantic just to look at a bridge. As for ruins, I know I ought to be intelligent about them, but they just make me think of nettles and weeds.'

The little party had drifted towards the entrance while she was talking. Suddenly she gave an exclamation. 'Why, just look at that!'

An old-fashioned carriage, of the open kind called a Victoria, was crawling slowly along the street. It was drawn by a chestnut horse, and its driver wore a bowler hat with a curly brim and had a metal number slung round his neck.

'Oh, that's just a cab.' Chris knew the sight well. 'The last cab in Edinburgh. It keeps on because tourists like to drive in it, but I think it's frightfully slow——'

'Do you mean it's for hire? Why, it looks just exactly like the Boston cabs in the old prints! Ambrose! We're certainly going in that cab!'

Chris felt dreadfully disappointed. She had looked forward so much to being taken for a run in the big flashing car which Pat had described. But Mr Bloomfield, who generally did what his wife asked him, had run down the steps and waved to the cab to stop. The cabman pulled up, giving an old-fashioned touch to his hat, and they all piled in.

Pat and Will looked rather embarrassed. They felt they were making public spectacles of themselves, displayed to the whole of Princes Street, as the cab turned and ambled slowly along it. They sat with their backs to the horses, and so could catch the expressions on the faces of the people they had just passed. Moreover, Chris had to squeeze in between Mr and Mrs Bloomfield, so the cab looked vulgarly full. Mr Bloomfield had put on a deadpan face. One couldn't tell whether he were enjoying himself or merely making the best of a bad job.

Only Mrs Bloomfield looked pleased and interested. Chris had seen the old man and his horse wandering about the streets all her life, and had often wondered what driving in it would be like. She had forgotten the Bentley for the moment. Mrs Bloomfield sat up very straight and bending a little forward, as the ladies in the old prints did. She wished she had a parasol to hold.

Nobody thought of giving any directions to the cabman. Somehow nobody dared, because the whole thing was like a dream where directions are never given, and things just happen without anyone's speaking a word. The horse slowed down to a walk and began to climb up the Mound. At the top it turned left and began gently ambling again, down the slower slope of the Royal Mile.

Then the cabman spoke. He had a gruff voice and he threw the words over his shoulder and made a jab with his whip. 'Heart o' Midlothian,' he said. They craned over the side of the vehicle to catch a glimpse of the large pattern of a heart laid out in cobblestones right in the middle of the empty space in front of St Giles' Cathedral.

'Law Courts and old House o' Parliament.' The Bloomfields had been over them already, so they just cast a glance into the elegant little square with its bronze statue in the middle. Down they went, lower and lower along the street, but now Mrs Bloomfield had opened her Guide and begun to annoy the old man very much by announcing what they were coming to before he was ready to tell them himself.

'Lady Ogilvie's House!' she announced triumphantly, waving the little red book towards the tall gaunt building with its crow-stepped gables.

'Naethin' o' the kind!' the cabman threw over his shoulder: 'it's Drumlie Close, that's what it is!'

Mrs Bloomfield flushed slightly. She prided herself upon the way she could follow maps and guides, and she cast a rapid eye down the list of names of the old houses, to make sure she had not made a mistake. There was no Drumlie Close mentioned along the whole length of the Royal Mile. She raised her voice, addressing the old man on the box.

'Excuse me, I think you're mistaken. According to my plan the house is called Lady Ogilvie's.'

'I dinna care what your plan says, it's Drumlie Close. That's what it was called when I was a laddie, and I'm no' goin' to learn new fancy names at my time o' life.'

Mr Bloomfield spoke for the first time since entering the cab. He always spoke when something needed to be smoothed over, particularly if it concerned his wife. 'I

A CAT AND A CLUE

guess a good many of the old names have been changed,' he said pacifically; adding, 'it's fine that some people still remember the old ones.'

This was evidently a sore subject with the cabman. 'Ay. The old ones were good enough for us. But folks are a' for fancy names and titles these days. Maybe some old woman calling hersel' Leddy Ogilvie spent a wheen years in yon house, but who minds her now? It wad be a drumlie place in her day, and it's drumlie yet. A fancy name 'll no' change it. Na!'

Mrs Bloomfield felt herself beaten, especially since she did not know what drumlie meant. Her eye caught a postcard-shop, and because she wanted both to change the subject and assert her authority, she said very sweetly and decidedly, 'I want to buy some postals to send to friends. Do you mind stopping a minute?'

The cab drew up to the curb. Pat decided that he would buy what Mrs Bloomfield called a 'postal' to send to a school friend in England, and Mr Bloomfield got out too because he felt cramped. The three of them went into the shop, leaving Chris still sitting among the navy-blue cushions with the leathery smell.

She looked at the cabman's broad back, and then at the dark houses towering above them on either side. The horse clawed at the cobbles with one iron shoe and hung his head down in the shafts. The cabman seemed to be muttering to himself. '. . . gone up and down the Mile this forty year,' he was saying, 'and nobody argued wi' me yet. Drumlie Close, that's what it is. Set them up wi' their Leddy Ogilvie, whoever *she* was! But there, when I'm gone, there'll be few enough left to remember the old name at a'!'

Chris felt she had to say something. 'Did they change many of the names?' she asked idly, her eyes on the shop door, watching for the others to come out.

'A wheen, here and there. First they dug oot some famous body who lived, maybe just a year or two, in one o' the houses. Dug it out o' books. Books! The lawyers are never done wi' them. And if it was a grand enough name, they'd ca' the place by it, till the old one dropped out and got forgotten, like the House o' the Pelican——'

'Wha—what did you say?' Chris could hardly believe she had heard the casual words. She scarcely noticed the others coming out of the shop again. They were climbing into the cab as the old man answered:

'And it wi' a pelican bird sculptured up on it as large as life! But no. Here they found that James the Sixth's Queen (Ann she was called) had paid it a visit the once. And so what must they do but ca' it Queen's Pleasure!'

'Queen's Pleasance!' Mrs Bloomfield interrupted excitedly. 'But *that's* in the guide book. I saw it!'

Mr Bloomfield was a quiet man, but his mind worked like lightning. Although he had only overheard half of the conversation, the mention of a pelican, and of an old name changed, was enough to tell him the whole story. There was a gleam behind his spectacles as he said, 'Drive us to Queen's Pleasance—at once!'

Chapter XIII

DEAD-END

THE cabby turned his horse round laboriously, stopping all traffic in the middle of the street until the operation was finished, and headed it back up the slope of the Royal Mile.

The boys looked at each other excitedly. 'Why, I guess we never thought of the name being changed!' Will exclaimed. 'No wonder nobody knew what we were talking about!'

Pat nodded. 'Of course old Lord Drumfingal called it the House of the Pelican because it was called that in his ancestors' time. But he said himself he didn't know even where it was; so he probably never heard about the new name.'

A slight uneasy doubt came into Pat's mind. 'All the same, you'd have thought people would remember the stone pelican and guess what house we wanted to find.'

'I don't know. People are apt to forget what they are accustomed to. Maybe no-one has bothered to look at the pelican for years and years.'

Mrs Bloomfield had opened a map on her knees. The wind ruffled it a bit as they drove along, and she had to hold it down with two hands. 'It's marked perfectly plainly—look! On the left-hand side of the road, near the Castle. Just opposite that place called the Outlook Tower. . . .'

A small cold premonition smote Pat. Yet where else

could the house be, for was it not from the Outlook Tower that they had seen Janet emerge into the street? He did not quite know what he feared, but all enthusiasm ebbed from him suddenly, and he could see, from Will's uneasy glance, that the American boy was thinking the same thing.

Neither Chris nor Mr Bloomfield had spoken a word. Chris was busy working out whether she could claim to have discovered the house which contained the golden box and, with it, the five hundred dollars payment for the job done. Visions of new mattresses billowed like striped clouds through her mind. Mr Bloomfield was calculating his chances of persuading the owner of the box to give it up, and how much he ought to offer him for it.

Nobody noticed St Giles or the Heart of Midlothian as they drove past them again. They were all too busy with their private thoughts and excitements, except perhaps Mrs Bloomfield, who had forgotten about the musical box and who was merely intent upon reading her map. The horse plodded across the tram-lines which cut through the Royal Mile, and began climbing the upper stretch of the road. Pat's heart sank lower, and Will began to look anxious, too. What they feared took place when the cabman, drawing up triumphantly before the high scaffolding, made a jab with his whip towards the boards entirely obscuring the frontages of the two old houses, and said, 'Yon's it!'

'What, in there?' Mr Bloomfield sprang from the cab on to the pavement. There was a gap in the boards just big enough to allow the workmen to pass in and out with their barrows and tools. He stepped over the rubble at the base of the gap, while the two boys followed him and Chris peered over his shoulder.

'It isn't there,' Pat told him; 'we've looked.'

Mr Bloomfield cast a swift eye upwards, over the stone fabric with its gaping windowless sockets. Neither a pelican nor anything else was there to ornament it. Janet had said it was over the entrance. But, like the other old houses along the Royal Mile, the entrances had obviously been at either side of these two, which were joined together, and a high wooden fence now pressed close to the stonework on both sides of the building, cutting off any courtyards that might have been flanking it.

Mr Bloomfield strode back to the cab. 'Which of them is the House of the Pelican?' he asked.

The cabman pointed again, this time to the right-hand house—or, rather, to the part of the scaffolding which obscured it. 'Yonder,' he said.

'The entrance to its yard would be at the side, I take it?'

'Aye. Wi' the stone pelican above, on a kind o' shield, like I told ye.'

'Well, it isn't visible now. What's more, a fence is clamped tight across it, cutting off any courtyard or entry there. How long has that fence been up?'

The old man scratched his head. 'Now, wad it be May or June they cleared oot the tenants? A matter o' months ago, onyway. Nae need o' an entry when there's nae folks to enter or leave.'

The boys and Mr Bloomfield looked at each other, bewildered. Mr Bloomfield stepped back through the space between the big hoardings to where he had seen two workmen sift a pile of rubble and dust. In a low voice (in case what he said might carry to the old man outside) he asked them if indeed the building had been fenced all that time.

'Aye,' one of the workmen replied; 'ye ken, we canna risk boys gettin' into the old houses after we leave every night. They wad think it a fine ploy, and break their necks on some rotten flooring.'

'There's a courtyard behind this, I suppose? As well as the two cut-off entries?'

'There's the old court. But naebody's trod it for months, seein' the only way in's boarded up. We're goin' to clear out the court too, when we get the main building finished.'

He picked up his wire-crossed frame and started sifting the rubble again, throwing the larger pieces on to a pile waiting to be carted away. Chris and the boys, who had followed Mr Bloomfield in and listened to what was said, now followed him out again, so confused that they said nothing at all. It was the big man who spoke as they stepped out into the street.

'Well,' he said, 'there goes all hope of the musical box. It's obvious that nobody could possibly be living in that house. Why, in parts you can see through it like a net! And Janet couldn't have got into the courtyard either—not as late as last week. It's been sealed off for months.'

'She—she was awfully sure about that pelican,' Chris put in.

'I guess what her brother said, to begin with, was right: that pelican was fabricated from the one she had seen in the Zoo. And if she ran through any courtyard, it wasn't the one behind here.'

DEAD-END

They climbed into the cab once more, very subdued. Real life closed in upon them again, and it seemed as though a lovely fantastic dream had vanished. How stupid they had been to believe it real! Only Mrs Bloomfield remained quite cheerful. She had allowed herself to believe in nothing but the map spread out on her knees.

Without being told the cabman had turned his horse to go back down the hill again. 'Yon brae's too steep for the beast,' he told them over his shoulder; adding, 'I'd no' have gone up it, but for your perseestance in wantin' to see yon house.'

They jogged more quickly down the Mound than they had gone up it, and were put down at the entrance to the North Caledonian Hotel. Mr Bloomfield gave the old man a handsome tip, and they all took leave of each other in a sort of deflated silence. It was time for Chris to hurry home and help her mother to get supper ready. Pat came with her, for want of anything better to do.

'I could wring Janet's neck,' he said rather savagely when they were half-way home.

Chris knew why he said it. He wasn't so much blaming his little sister for making up one of her usual stories, as blaming himself for expecting it to be true. She felt rather sorry for Janet. After all, no-one would have taken the story seriously if it hadn't been for that odd series of coincidences. First, the coincidence of finding that there *was* a place called the House of the Pelican. Then Janet's knowing how to set the bird-box going; and then the cabman's being able to take them to the place. . . .

'Mr Bloomfield seems dreadfully disappointed,' she said, 'especially about not finding that musical box. I must say it was queer how Janet touched the right knob to set it going.'

'Oh, that was just a lucky chance,' Pat replied, shrugging his shoulders.

Chris said nothing more until they had let themselves into the house. But all the time, at the back of her mind, she felt there had been too many lucky chances to be quite natural. Of course the thing was ridiculous; there was *no* way of getting into, or near, the old house. As she walked slowly upstairs she seemed to see it rise up once more before her eyes. The roof had been off, she remembered, and the blue sky had shone through the empty holes in the fabric where once the windows had been.

As for the courtyard behind it, the two entrances had been completely blocked off from the street for months. Yet the stone pelican must be over one of them. It had to be there, if Janet had really seen it at all, for she couldn't have seen through the scaffolding facing the street.

Had Janet made up the whole story, or had she run in and out of the rabbit-warren of little lanes and yards, led by that band of children, until she had become thoroughly muddled, and had perhaps seen the old man and the staircase and the little gold box somewhere else?

It was worth trying to find out. And she was given the opportunity a few minutes later, when her mother, hearing her come upstairs, leaned over the bannisters and called down, 'Is that you Chris? The Mathesons rang up to ask me to go to the theatre with them. I'll need to leave early, so maybe you'll put Janet to bed after supper. Just leave the dishes. The woman can do them tomorrow.'

At supper Janet was very annoyed to hear that they

had ridden in the cab without her. She had seen that old cab, she said, and when Pat said there was no room for another person anyway, she was sure the cabman would have let her sit beside him and perhaps even hold the whip. Even the Bonds were interested in the drive, so Pat told them all about it; but Chris noticed that he never mentioned their hunt for the House of the Pelican.

Mrs MacKendrick looked quite pretty that night, pretty and flushed with pleasure at the thought of going to see some of the Festival. She hadn't been told what the play was, but her tastes were the same as Will Bloomfield's, and she rather hoped that it wasn't Shakespeare. She had put on her best dress and the pair of paste earrings shaped like little half-moons that Chris had given her for her last birthday. Now and then, as she ate, she looked across at her daughter apologetically; but Chris smiled brightly back to show that she didn't mind being left behind.

When they had finished supper and Mrs MacKendrick had gone, Mrs Bond helped Chris to collect the dishes and stack them at the side of the scullery sink. The Bonds did not give an evening performance, as their entertainment was mostly for children and they gave matinées every afternoon. Mrs Bond even offered to put Janet to bed, but Chris had her own reasons for wanting to do it herself.

She filled the bath for her, and even put in a drop of some rather strong scent from a small phial she treasured and only used occasionally. She wanted Janet to be in a good temper to answer questions. Janet sniffed appreciatively when she entered the bathroom, and promised to wash well behind the ears. Chris made down her bed while she was having her bath, and presently Janet came into the room again, wearing the pink dressing-gown

Mrs Browning, in London, had chosen for her, and the slippers with large silk pom-poms she had chosen for herself.

'Will that scent be strong enough to last?' Janet tucked herself into bed and sniffed again to make sure it was still there.

'I should think so. It cost one and six. Janet, listen. You know that time you followed Effie into the yard behind the old house? The time you saw the stone pelican?'

Janet scowled. She had heard enough about it, and had enough scoldings, too. 'I did see it,' she muttered.

'Maybe you did,' Chris hastened to reassure her. 'Only perhaps you got muddled after you met those children. Because, you know, there isn't any way into that court. Not from the street.'

Then Janet said a surprising thing; said it quite casually, as if she had told everyone before or had just forgotten to mention it because it wasn't important: 'Effie didn't go straight into it from the street. Not into the yard where the little wooden staircase was. She went by a little sort of winding way and I followed her. I hid behind the big ash bins, like I said. I was afraid to come out at once, when she went away——'

'But the children showed you the way out? Perhaps they ran into the court and you followed them out?' Chris held her breath, waiting for Janet's reply.

Janet shook her head. 'Nobody came in. There was only the old man up in the roof. I got frightened and wanted to go back and ask him the way out. Then I heard people singing, quite near. And I went to where the singing was, and there was a big girl with funny teeth, and they threw a ball . . .' Janet yawned. She wasn't interested any more.

'How did you get to where they were playing? Don't settle down—you can't be as sleepy as all that!' Chris said desperately. She felt she was on the edge of something important; something that might clear up the whole mystery, and there was Janet pulling the blankets up to her ears, with her eyes half-closed already!

''Cos I heard them singing.' Janet began to sing sleepily herself:

> *The wind, the wind, the wind blows high,*
> *The snow comes tumbling from the sky,*
> *And Maisie Paterson's going to die*
> *For want of the golden city.*

'Janet! Was Maisie Paterson the girl with the funny teeth? Did she show you the way out?'

Janet nodded sleepily. 'She threw the ball and it hit me. She didn't see me coming. She said, "Hullo kid! Lost yourself?" And I picked up the ball, and she let me play——'

'How near was the singing to the House of the Pelican? Quite close? Was she surprised to see you coming from it? Did she know the way in?'

Chris tumbled the words out one after the other. But there was no answer from Janet. Her long black lashes had fluttered down. She was asleep.

Chapter XIV

MAISIE PATERSON

CHRIS, however, took a long while to go to sleep that night.

She lay in the darkness, going over and over what Janet had said. Here, she felt sure, lay the clue which would reveal the secret of the old house at last. She belonged to Edinburgh herself, and she knew that behind the Royal Mile there lay a network of little lanes and passages, mostly unused except by the gangs of children who played in them, ran through them, had their own names for them until they grew up and went away or forgot them because they played there no longer.

Once, long ago when she was little, she had run away from her mother on the Mound, and had been lost in those passages herself. But she had encountered some rough boys, and they had thrown stones at her until she had run, sobbing, out of the narrow lane by which she had entered, and a policeman had seen her and taken her home.

She had been slapped quite hard by her agitated mother, and forbidden ever to go there again. She had never wanted to, she had been too frightened. But she remembered distinctly the maze of little courts and passages leading between them, and for a long while afterwards her nightmares consisted of running down Black Man's Tunnel, with the boys at her heels and stones whizzing past her ankles. . . .

Black Man's Tunnel. . . . She had forgotten the name, but now it came back to her. 'After her! She's awa' doon Black Man's Tunnel!' one of the boys had shouted as they pursued her. It was old Mr Smith who had been so interested when she had told him that. Old Mr Smith, who was one of their first boarders, and who knew everything about the Royal Mile.

Old Mr Smith had said there was once an inn called the Negro's Head somewhere behind the Royal Mile. Even its site had long been forgotten, but he said the name Black Man's Tunnel was probably a—what did he call it?—a local memory, still lingering about the place. The people who lived near where it had once stood wouldn't remember anything about the inn itself. But they had their own names for places, no matter whether the Town Council changed them or not. Sometimes they would stick to the old name while people just a little farther up the street had adopted the new one.

Old Mr Smith had become quite excited about Black Man's Tunnel. He was writing a book about the Royal Mile, and he hadn't been able to find just where the Negro's Head had been. He wanted to take Chris back there to show him the passage, but Mrs MacKendrick hadn't allowed it, and Chris herself hadn't wanted to go.

Soon after that, old Mr Smith had died before even finishing his book. It was a pity, because perhaps he might have known the old name of the house now called Queen's Pleasance, and whether there were any passages leading to its courtyard from the back. Now only the children might know of such a passage, because children round about there swarmed like rabbits and went where tourists and grown-ups never bothered to go.

Girls for instance, like Maisie Paterson. . . .

She fell asleep at last, but only to dream that she was a little girl again, much nearer the pavement and running hard across it to escape from the boys pursuing her. There was the dark little passage just facing her, and she was diving into it like a rabbit, while, as if from very far away came the echoing shout from behind her, ' She's awa' doon Black Man's Tunnel ! ' Now she was running down it towards the spot of light at the end. But when she reached the end she was trapped, because a huge pelican stood in the exit ; a real pelican, not one carved in stone, and its great strong beak pointed right towards her. . . .

She woke unrefreshed. But by the time she had dressed the dream had receded, and she knew what she was going to do. As soon as breakfast was finished she signalled to Pat. ' Come upstairs to the drawing-room,' she whispered. ' I've something I want to say to you.'

The big cold room with its decorated furniture was always empty at this time of day. Pat followed her there, wondering what she had to tell him. ' Look here,' she said abruptly, ' you remember what Mr Bloomfield said ? About giving five hundred dollars to anyone who could find out where Janet's old man with the gold box lived?'

Pat nodded. 'But we can't. We've looked, and personally I'm sure she made up the whole thing.'

'Well, I don't want to be mean or steal a march on anyone. Supposing—supposing there *was* an old man, and one of us found him, we wouldn't need to tell the others, would we?'

Pat grasped what she meant at once. 'You mean, you wouldn't need to split the " pay for the job "? Of course not. We've all tried, and we can all try again, separately or together. So far as I'm concerned I've given it up, and so has Will. We're not going to waste any more time; but if you like to, you're welcome.'

'If I did find him, you wouldn't grudge me the money or think I was mean?'

'Don't be silly. If you think you've a clue, go straight ahead. *Have* you a clue?'

'I think I have,' she said slowly.

He felt violently tempted to ask what it was. She saw what he was thinking and added in a hurry, 'If it is a clue at all, it's something both you and Will could have found out too. I don't know anything more than you both could have found out if you'd liked. That's why I think I should have the five hundred dollars.'

Pat laughed kindly. 'Go right ahead! We shan't grudge it to you, and you needn't tell us anything if you don't want to. But I'd almost bet the whole five hundred dollars that you'll just find Janet has taken you in.'

It was laundry morning, and she had to help her mother to strip the beds and count the sheets. However, Mrs MacKendrick was feeling a little guilty at having enjoyed herself so much the night before, and was more than willing to let Chris feel free to do what she liked after lunch. ' Go out and get some fresh air,' she urged. ' Why not go down to the swimming-pool at Portobello ? I'm sure Isabel Mathieson would go with you.'

But Chris didn't want to take her school friend Isabel, or anyone else for that matter, where she was going that afternoon. So she just muttered vaguely, and after the midday meal was over she put on her oldest coat and went out as quickly as she could before anyone should tell her to tidy herself. Where she was going, she didn't want to look tidy. She felt, somehow, that it might frighten Maisie Paterson off.

She went first to a shop which sold games and children's toys. One had to have something to approach Maisie Paterson with, and she had thought up a good excuse. She looked first at the rubber balls, painted different colours, but decided that they were far too childish. Janet had distinctly said that Maisie Paterson was a big girl. What sort of a ball, then, would she have been playing with ? Surely some ball she had picked up from somewhere, and not just a child's toy. . . .

Something like an old tennis ball. She went to the sports department and bought one reluctantly, because the painted kind were so much cheaper. The tennis ball looked far too new. It would not do for her purpose unless it were dirtied and used. She turned off Princes Street and entered some gardens which lay behind it a little way down the hill. The gardens lay, cool and shady, with big trees which hid them from the windows of the houses lying all around. Only a few old people sat about on chairs, and all was comparatively empty. Chris was glad to notice this, for she felt she looked ' daft ' playing ball all by herself, a big girl of her age.

She chose the loneliest part of the gardens, and hurled the ball across the flower bed once or twice. It bounced through the earth and became nicely soiled. Then she aimed at a tree trunk which looked rather sooty, and flung the ball against it again and again. Now the ball was quite dirty ; scratched as well ; it looked as though it had been played with for ages. She picked it up, gave it a glance of satisfaction, and shoved it into her pocket, telling herself that her coat needed cleaning anyway, so what did it matter ?

It was a hot day. The sun reached even to the Royal Mile, shining white on one side of the street and casting inky shadows over the other. Chris turned to the right along the steep street, keeping her eyes well open for children playing before the old houses. But the traffic was busy that afternoon ; buses and cars thundered up towards the Castle, since this was the popular hour for tourists to visit it. All to the good. The children must be somewhere about, since it was holiday time, and it would be easier to find Maisie Paterson and talk to her in one of the quiet courtyards behind the houses facing the street.

The workmen were emptying a barrowful of sand in the cleared space behind the scaffolding masking the two old houses. She heard the creak of the lorry as it tilted back, and then the thud of the sand, and looked through the opening as she walked past. Then she retraced her steps to look at something which had not been there before. It was a sort of iron tripod with a great metal ball hanging from it at the end of a chain. As she watched a man swung the chain, and the ball crashed sullenly into the crumbling stonework against which it was aimed. A shower of soot-covered rubble slid to the ground, and a great crack suddenly appeared like a vein on the surface of the building.

She watched fascinated. The ball was swung again and again, showing a larger area of whitened exposed surface, while the crack now spread ominously right under what had once been a window. The workman swinging the chain saw her, and gave her a smile.

'Watch out, lassie!' he called. 'Yon whole gable might give way ony moment!'

She stepped back hastily towards the street. 'Are you taking it down?'

'Just the stonework round the window and a bit o' the wall at the side. But the whole building's unsafe, and ye never ken. If 'twas me, I'd dynamite the lot, but it's what they ca' an ancient monument, so we've to go cannily and leave as much up as'll stay.'

He seemed to have finished with the iron ball, for he let it clang into stillness against the tripod.

'That's a queer thing.' Chris pointed towards the ball.

'Have ye never seen a Sheer-Legs afore? That's what we ca' it. We use it to make a wee breach, or to weaken the fabric. Then comes the pick-axe, if the whole building's no' to come doon.'

He lifted a pick-axe from the side of a pile of rubble and walked towards the half-ruined gable-end of the house. He inserted it in the crack and pulled gently. Two or three stones came out like blackened teeth, and he cleared them away with his foot. Sometimes he swung the axe, giving quite a hard blow. Sometimes he merely wiggled the point gently between two stones still in place, and then little puffs of old mortar came spraying out.

He had his back to her now, paying no more attention. She remembered Maisie Paterson again, felt the ball in her pocket, and walked on past the scaffolding towards the next entry along the street farther up. Sure enough, there were children playing somewhere behind it; she could hear the echo of their rough hoarse voices as she began to walk down the covered passage towards them.

But when she came out into the yard she saw they were only small children, and Maisie Paterson was not there. At least there was no girl bigger than the others with crossed teeth. They had drawn chalk lines on the

THE HOUSE OF THE PELICAN

pavement, and were shoving a square piece of stone across them with the side of one foot; playing a sort of hop-scotch called Peever.

They paid no attention to her whatever. She stood watching for a moment or two, and then called out, 'Does anybody know where Maisie Paterson is?'

They stopped the game, staring. 'What d'ye want wi' her?' one red-haired child asked suspiciously.

'Never you mind. Where is she?'

'I dinna ken.' The child pushed the stone over one of the lines. It was obvious that the game was going to begin again, and that Maisie Paterson wasn't anywhere around.

'Listen,' Chris almost shouted, she was so anxious to hold their attention: 'does anyone know the way in to the House of the Pelican?'

Dead silence. A very dirty little boy with a school cap over one ear gave her a sudden sly look—the others had put on dumb expressions. He at least looked as if he knew what she was talking about. She leaned forward swiftly and grabbed hold of his arm by the ragged jersey which covered it, drawing him to her side.

'There's a stone bird with a big beak carved on it, and a yard like this and a wee wooden staircase—now, do you know what I'm talking about?'

She was sure somehow that he did; but his eyes only slid towards the others, and she thought that they hid a flicker of fear. With her free hand she felt in the pocket other to the one holding the ball. She remembered that there had been a bag of boiled sweets in it last time she wore the coat. It was still there. She showed him the bag.

Leaning over the sill and laughing

MAISIE PATERSON

'I want to see the stone bird. You can have these sweeties if you show me where it is.'

'I canna. I'm feared.' Still, he eyed the bag as he spoke.

'Oh, you're feared, are you?' She tried to sound contemptuous as she held the bag out so that the other children could see it. 'Maybe somebody else'll take me then.'

The children crept forward until they enclosed her in a ring. They all stared at the bag which she held high in the air so that no-one could snatch it from her. The little boy wriggled in her grasp. 'Let me go,' he said sullenly. 'I'm no' wantin' to see the old witch.'

'What old witch?'

'The one that lives in yon court. I'm no' goin' there. I'm feared o' her.'

'You're a silly wee fool. There's no such thing, I tell you!'

A small girl interrupted her hotly. 'There is so! She kens a' the cats in the place, and they come visitin' her after dark. I've seen them!'

'Don't be daft! Have you seen the witch?'

'Na! But I've seen the cats. Dozens o' them, a' chasin' across the street an' climbin' doon the roofs, makin' for the wee passage into Pelican Court as soon as it's dark! It's then that she feeds them——'

'How do you know, if you've never seen her?' Chris asked her sharply.

''Cos they come oot wi' bits o' fish in their mouths. Give me thae sweeties!'

'Not till you take me into Pelican Court. Whichever one of you——'

The boy gave a sudden wriggle and jerked himself free. A taller boy sprang up and snatched the paper bag out of her hand. It tore, but most of the sweets stayed in his hand. With a shout of triumph he ran away, followed by the others like a pack at his heels. They vanished down the little passage leading into the street. In one moment the yard had emptied, leaving Chris standing in the middle of it alone.

She felt dazed and angry. Also, she felt a fool and hoped that nobody had been watching how they had tricked her. She peered upward, examining the row upon row of dirty windows ringing the court around. They were mostly empty at this time of day, but five or six storeys up she saw a girl almost her own age leaning over the sill and laughing.

It was rough coarse laughter, and it made her feel angrier still; but then she remembered that the girl might be useful after all. So she shouted up towards her, 'Do you know where Maisie Paterson is?'

'I'm Maisie Paterson. What d'ye want wi' me?'

It was her first stroke of luck that day. 'I want to talk to you,' she shouted back.

'Wait then, and I'll come down.'

The window slammed. Chris stood there waiting for what seemed a very long time. But the Patersons' flat was high up, and the twisting old stone staircase took a long while to land anyone at the bottom. There was nobody in the yard now at all. All was suddenly quiet—so quiet Chris imagined she could hear Maisie's footsteps travelling down and down. . . .

Chapter XV

THE DISAPPEARANCE OF EFFIE

THERE were so many entries to so many stairways, Chris could not guess which one would bring Maisie out. When the girl did appear she walked out of one that Chris had scarcely noticed. She was a tall girl, and had made some attempt to be tidier than the younger children who had been in the court; but there was a wild untamed look about her too, though her grin, as she approached, was friendly enough. Chris noticed that her two front teeth were crossed, just as Janet had said.

Maisie was standing in front of her now. 'What d'ye want?' she said.

Chris pulled the ball out of her pocket. 'Is this yours?' she asked.

Maisie's hand went out half-way towards it, then drew back. 'What made ye think I'd lost it?' she asked suspiciously.

Chris was careful to speak the truth and not to add anything. 'Oh,' she said vaguely, 'a wee girl I know, called Janet, was playing in here the other day. She was playing Golden City with a ball, and it bounced out into the street. You can have this one if you like.'

Maisie's eyes narrowed. 'Did she send ye back with it?'

Chris spoke more vaguely still. 'She'd wandered into the yard in front of the House of the Pelican. It's near here somewhere, isn't it? She sort of got lost, but you found her and played with her. I want to give you the ball.'

Where Maisie lived nobody gave away anything for nothing. Chris had thought that bringing the ball was a good idea and would give her a reason for wanting to see Maisie. But it only made the other girl suspicious.

'What is it ye're wantin'?' she merely repeated, and did not put out her hand for the ball.

'Here, take it, even if it isn't yours,' Chris said still more foolishly ; adding, 'it's a good ball though it has got a bit dirty.'

'Ye'll be wantin' something in exchange, I ken that fine !' Maisie gave her a cunning glance. 'Or else ye wadna' come speirin' here——'

Chris lost her temper. 'I'm offering you a perfectly good ball in exchange for one simple little thing !'

'What's that?'

'I want to see the stone pelican Janet told me about. You know, the big bird carved over the doorway to that old house in the yard. The—the one with the wee wooden staircase.'

Maisie's eyes had been greedily fixed on the ball. One hand had almost gone out to take it. Now she jerked it back, and her eyes became empty of all expression. 'I'm no' wantin' your ball,' she said sulkily. 'I'm too big to play wi' such trash !'

Chris was now roused and desperate. 'Don't you pretend there isn't such a place!' she shouted. 'Because there is! There is! Yon wee boy who was here a few minutes ago told me. He said an old witch lived in it, and he wouldn't take me there——'

Maisie took a step back, looking rather frightened. 'Keep your hair on!' she muttered. 'Maybe there *is* such a place, but I'm no' takin' ye to it. No' for ony ball!'

"'Fraid cat, that's what you are! Afraid of the old witch like the wee children half your age!'

'I'm no' feared!' Maisie shot back indignantly; 'there's no such things as witches, and I wadna' believe in them if there was!'

'All right, go on, take me to the House of the Pelican or I'll think you a coward! A coward, a coward!'

A red flush of rage crept up to the roots of Maisie's hair. 'What's that ye say?' She advanced threateningly. 'Say it again!'

Chris gulped but stood her ground. 'I say you're a coward to be afraid of witches. Why else won't you take me to see the house?'

'Go on, ye wee fool! There's no such place!'

'Yes there is; you said so yourself. All the children who play here know it. They told me they did. If you won't take me, I'll find one who will. And *he'll* get the ball!'

To her delight she saw an uncertain look come into the other girl's face. 'I can tak' ye myself,' Maisie said sullenly; adding, 'but ye'll need to give me something better than an old ball.'

'I haven't any money with me. I don't get much

pocket money really, but I could come back with . . .' Her voice trailed away. She realised that this might be her only chance. Once let Maisie away to think things over, and she might never find her again.

But Maisie's eyes had been fixed on the lapel of her coat for some time. 'Ye can give me yon brooch. It's real bonny.'

'What brooch?' Chris squinted down, and caught sight of the little silver one set with cairngorms she had pinned on last time she had worn the coat, and then had forgotten about. It was a favourite piece of hers, and she felt very reluctant to part with it; but there was nothing else to do, so she nodded. 'All right then. You can have the brooch if you take me to the House of the Pelican.'

'Hand us it then.'

Chris shook her head firmly. 'Not till we get there. Do you think I'm daft?'

Now that she had made up her mind all Maisie's wrath seemed to have vanished. She gave a cheerful grin which showed her crooked teeth, and said, 'Come on wi' ye. And keep close, for it's awful easy to lose yourself where we're goin'.'

She beckoned Chris across the courtyard again, glancing up at the windows as she went. 'It's in the bit that's closed to the public,' she confided, 'because of the old houses they're takin' down round about. We're no' allowed to go there, so mind and keep it to yourself!'

They entered a narrow alley-way between two buildings. The houses on either side were still occupied, for clothes-pulleys stretched between them, and garments flapped over their heads. They crossed the yard beyond, where some children were playing, but Maisie paid no

THE DISAPPEARANCE OF EFFIE

attention to them. Now she led Chris right through the arched entrance to another old house, and out at a door, ancient and iron-studded, leading on to a little lane beyond.

It was very quiet in the lane. Here all the houses looked empty and tumbling down. No doubt the demolition squad would reach them presently, and Chris suddenly found herself wishing with all her heart that she could hear the comforting sound of men working at hand. For here she could hear nothing at all. Not a footstep, not a child's voice, not even the scream of a sea-gull flying overhead. Nothing but the sound of their own passage between the high blind walls.

Instinctively she stood still and listened. Even the traffic on the Royal Mile had failed to reach this length. They must be somewhere in no-man's land; in the forgotten quarter where nobody went because now nobody lived there any more. But the House of the Pelican must lie just behind the big scaffolding, and that was quite near to the Royal Mile. For the first time a suspicion of Maisie shot into her mind.

'Where are you taking me to?' she cried.

At the same moment Maisie seemed to lurch sideways, falling against her and grabbing her as though to steady herself. Chris felt a jerk at her coat, and the next moment the girl had sprung away, triumphant, with the brooch in her hand.

'Find the way yourself!' she cried, turning on her heel and beginning to run back along the lane. Chris immediately ran after her and saw her disappear through the iron-studded door which stood ajar. By the time she had reached the inhabited courtyard beyond it, however, Maisie had vanished from sight.

Chris stood in the middle of the yard, wondering what to do next. She was so angry at the way she had been tricked she found she couldn't even think clearly. She had lost her sense of direction too, and could not even remember by which of the many openings ringing round the court they had come. If she took one of them she might find herself in the Grassmarket, or anywhere. . . .

She was completely lost.

And then, as she stood there, she heard the sound of a woman's voice coming faintly from somewhere beyond the yard, but travelling nearer and nearer. It was raised in a sing-song call; a call familiar to everyone in Edinburgh, and particularly to Chris, who always looked out for it in Caroline Square on Thursdays. . . .

'Caller-oo! Caller-oo!'

It was the call of the fishwives from Leith, and one of them must be making her rounds of the tall old houses,

THE DISAPPEARANCE OF EFFIE

penetrating into the yards in order to sell her fish. As the signal-call drew nearer, windows were opened high above Chris. Women leaned over their window-sills, watching one of the entrances. Chris felt inclined to call up to them herself, and ask the way back to the Royal Mile. Then she decided that it would be simpler to wait a few moments and ask the fishwife when she appeared.

She stepped back into the shelter of the archway, so as to get a good view of all the other entrances. She was in deep shadow herself, but the sun shone white on the courtyard, almost hurting her eyes. The queer harsh call came nearer, holding the last note so that it carried far. And now she saw a glimmer of blue skirts appear in the crushed-up passage between the two buildings opposite. The fishwife stepped into the yard, bent a little forward with the weight of the creel on her back.

It was Effie.

Chris never knew what had stopped her from coming out of the shadows and speaking to Effie. Maybe an idea had begun to dawn in her mind even then. At any rate she stood still, watching, while the women at the windows shouted down and Effie shouted up.

'Have ye ony fresh haddies the day?'

'Aye. Plenty. And a nice big cod.'

'I'm no' wantin' the cod. Come away up wi' the haddies. I'll take them and maybe a herring or two.'

Effie disappeared into the doorway of one of the houses. The heads of the women disappeared from the windows. They were evidently preparing to receive her at their doors. It was a very tall house, and Chris guessed that it would take Effie quite a while to stop at all the flats piled high on top of each other, to sell her wares. She stood there waiting for the woman to come down again. And as she stood, she had time to think out clearly what had flashed into her mind the moment the fishwife had come into view.

It was somewhere about here that the boys had tried to follow Effie and had lost her before. It was somewhere about here that the House of the Pelican was. And Pat had been sure that Effie knew where it was. She might even be on her way there now. At any rate Effie knew of some short-cut back to the Royal Mile, so it would be a good plan to follow her and see where she went first. . . .

But she was sure to cross the courtyard again and go up the winding stone stairs at whose foot Chris was standing now. There were lots of flats in this old house too, and voices had hailed her from above where Chris stood. She took a step out of the shadows and looked quickly round the yard. There was an old stone out-house standing at a corner of it. She ran across the yard, slipped behind the little low building and peeped round the corner of it.

A few minutes later Effie stepped out into the yard again, and, crossing it, disappeared into the shadowy archway of the house opposite. Six or seven dusty and broken windows, one above the other, lit the old stone staircase up which she travelled, from one flight to the next. Chris could watch her slow passage, because the blue skirts brushed against the windows, travelling higher and higher, disappearing for a few minutes as she reached each landing and paused at each doorway to sell her fish.

Now she was coming down again. She came down much quicker than she had gone up, for she made no halt, and her blue skirts appeared and reappeared at the staircase windows with only slight pauses when she negotiated the

THE DISAPPEARANCE OF EFFIE

steps in between. Chris saw her pass the first storey, and waited for her to step out through the shadows into the sun; but the seconds passed and still there was no sign of her. Nor was there a basement flat at which Effie might have been delayed. . . .

She edged cautiously out from behind the shed, staring towards the archway which hid the foot of the steps. What on earth had happened to Effie? Had she just sat down on the bottom step for a rest, or maybe twisted her ankle and wasn't able, with the heavy creel on her back, to get up without help?

She felt that she had to know. Besides, it wouldn't be kind to leave Effie stiting there, helpless, with a lot of fish on her back. The idea that she *might* have been going on to the House of the Pelican was such a fantastic one that Chris felt ashamed, now, of her childish wish to prevent Effie from seeing her. The fishwife could at least tell her how to get back to the Royal Mile. She did not hesitate longer, but ran over to the dark hooded entrance and glanced at the foot of the stairs.

They were quite empty. Effie was not there.

She could not believe her eyes. The fishwife had certainly not climbed up the stairway again, or Chris would have seen her against the windows. There wasn't the door of a flat in sight, for the staircase twisted steeply upward from the worn stone floor of the entrance towards an invisible landing above. Chris could feel a strong draught curl about her ankles as she stood there. The iron-studded outer door—the one just under the archway, giving on to the lane where Maisie had abandoned her—stood widely ajar letting in a cool current of air from the lane itself.

Surely she hadn't left that door so wide open when she ran through it a few minutes ago?

And then she knew in a flash where Effie had gone. She darted through it herself, and was just in time to catch a glimpse of the fishwife's great bobbing basket as it disappeared down the bottom of the lane.

Chapter XVI

THROUGH THE FENCE

CHRIS was glad she was wearing crêpe-soled shoes which made little noise as she ran down the lane. The faint sullen echo of the fishwife's footsteps still guided her when she stood still for a moment to listen. Ahead of her the lane gave a sharp turn to the left. She went more cautiously as she approached the turn, and halted after she had rounded it, in case Effie should be in sight and look round.

She was in sight, but she did not look round. Obviously she never dreamed that anyone else was about in this desolate place. For the lane ended only in an abandoned patch of sour grass, which must have once been used as a washing-green by the empty houses standing around it. A few rusty iron poles still stood erect in the middle of the patch of grass, and a sodden piece of washing-rope lay beneath them. The backs of two houses stood looking down on it. Both owned gaping sockets where the windows had been, and one was roofless already, its rafters showing like black ribs against the sky. They were obviously in the process of either demolition or reconstruction, but the work must be progressing from the other side of them, since nothing showed here but a high fence cutting them off from the deserted green.

There were a good many cats about the green. Two sat on the fence, and a third, a slinking yellow creature with a hungry eye, leaped, startled, from almost under Chris's foot and ran away snarling and spitting. She scarcely noticed them however. She was intent upon watching what Effie was doing at the other end of the green.

The big woman had gone down on her knees on the grass and was feeling up and down the fence with her hands. It was almost as if she expected to take it apart like a toy, and, indeed, in a moment she had lifted a plank right out and laid it neatly down on the ground beside her. The plank next to it was also loose, for she lifted that out too without any difficulty. Then she pushed her basket endways through the gap, and followed it by squeezing through herself.

Chris ran hastily across the grass and looked through the hole in the fence. Instantly a little square picture sprang to the eye as though framed in wood. The fence formed the fourth side of a small courtyard which contained nothing but two enormous and rusted ash-bins. Straight opposite her there was a wooden staircase leading to what seemed to be a separate little dwelling stuck on to the main building like a limpet, and reached by a door at the top of the staircase. There was a small shuttered window on either side of the door. The proper entry to the courtyard was to the left, but it had been boarded up

A separate little dwelling

apparently quite recently, since the wood looked fresh and white by contrast to the blackened stone of the archway. A blurred bit of carving showed on the stone. It was the figure of a pelican, almost defaced by weather and time....

The House of the Pelican ! That must be it, that hulk towering above the little room with its arched supports under it ; that closed and silent building straight opposite and endwise to the two other houses upon which workmen had already been busy. For Chris was suddenly aware of the sounds of men at work somewhere beyond the boarded-up entry. There were voices, and hammering, and now and then a sharp fall of stones. They must be working round at the front of the building. And she knew now just where it was. It was one of the two facing the Royal Mile behind the high scaffolding. Now, when she listened, she could even hear the rattle of the buses running down towards the Mound.

The lane, with its sharp turn, had led right back towards the street. All this flashed into her mind in an instant, while she was watching what Effie did next. Effie had put the strap of the basket once more round her brow and was clambering with it up the small wooden staircase. When she reached the top she knocked sharply on one of the shuttered windows. 'Caller-oo !' she called, but softly this time, as though she was afraid that the sound of her voice would carry too far.

The shutter swung outward, and an old man's head appeared. He was a very untidy old man with a fretful expression. 'Did ye bring me yon lobster ye promised !' he asked.

The yard was so small that Chris, peering from behind the fence, could hear every word. 'I couldna' get one,'

Effie was saying; 'but I've brought ye a flounder or two.'

'Aweel,' sighed the old man, watching while she unhitched the basket and rooted about in it for the flounders, 'I'm fair sick o' fish and that's a fact. I'd thought a lobster would be a wee change.'

'Did Maisie no' manage to get ye the sausages?' Effie produced the fish and handed them through the window.

'Aye, but she forgot the fat to fry them wi'. I had to boil them, and boiled sausages just taste like flannel. Wait you till I get the money.'

He jerked backwards again like a marionette, and the window was empty once more. When he reappeared Chris heard the chink of money passing between them. Then the old man spoke once more. He spoke always in a complaining way, like the sob of a small wind going down an empty passage.

'My watch has stopped again. Can ye tak' it to the watch-menders for me?'

She shook her head. 'It's his half-day, and I'll no' be round again till next Thursday. Better give it to Maisie. She's a careful lass, and she'll get it done for ye.'

'Aweel.' He gave another gusty sigh. 'Thank ye for bringing the fish onyway. If it wasna' for you and Maisie I'd starve.'

Effie stooped and lifted the big basket, slinging it on to her back. 'Ye're a great fool, John Jamieson, that's what ye are! D'ye no' ken the house isn't safe? The house-breakers may come here ony day to bring it about your ears!'

'I'll bide where I am till they do. I have my reasons.'

THROUGH THE FENCE

The shutter over the window suddenly slammed. Effie turned and began to go down the steps again. Chris, seeing her coming, dodged away from the fence and began running as hard as she could over the grass and into the lane, hoping to reach it before Effie had got through the fence. Half-way down the lane she glanced over her shoulder, and was glad to see that the fishwife was not yet in sight. She swept round the bend like a swallow, dashed through the old door at the end of it, and had taken up her place behind the little outhouse in the courtyard beyond, well before Effie appeared.

The fishwife trod heavily across the yard and turned into a different passage from the one she had entered it by. Following cautiously behind her, Chris managed to keep her in sight until the recurring roar of the Royal Mile showed they were just about to converge on it. Then she slowed up, and arrived at the entrance and the pavement outside by the time the streams of people passing down from the Castle had blotted Effie from sight.

It did not matter. She could find her way home now quite well. By this time it was late afternoon, and a cool wind blew in from the Firth, wiping away the dust and heat of the day. Excitement and triumph prevented Chris from realising how far she had walked and run, and how tired she was. A sort of bubbling-up feeling filled her veins, and she hardly minded the further walk down the Mound, for she had nothing left in her pocket to pay for a tram.

Besides, it would bring her down into Princes Street, and there was a big furniture shop with a display of mattresses in the window. She wanted to price them. All the afternoon concerts and theatre matinées had just

THE HOUSE OF THE PELICAN

given up their audiences, so the great street was filled with a moving mass from end to end. Chris glanced at the faces as they surged past her. Many looked strange and foreign, but their strangeness wasn't any greater than that of the discovery she had just made. Americans with wide hats and pale suits strolled past; an Indian lady wore scarlet and silver, with a little red spot on her forehead to show she was a Hindoo; and a group of French sailors off a ship in the Firth strolled along with the queer pompoms on their caps bobbing as they talked. . . .

They were no stranger than the little old man who lived with his golden box in the House of the Pelican. And she, Chris, alone, had discovered him. He was real, not just something imagined by Janet. For one heart-stopping moment she wondered if Janet had made up the golden box? But no, she had known where the hidden spring was in the other one at the exhibition.

There *was* a gold box. That meant five hundred dollars, and new mattresses for every bed in the house—and here were the mattresses themselves. Chris stood still with her nose glued to the window, reading the price tabs. Pat had to speak to her twice and touch her arm before she realised that he was standing just behind her.

He and Janet and Mrs Bloomfield. Chris was disappointed not to see Mr Bloomfield, but after all perhaps it was just as well. She could hardly blurt out where she had been in front of the others. They might then insist upon coming too, and make themselves eligible for part of the prize. Janet, for instance, might very well say that she had found the House of the Pelican first. Of course that was a very different thing from leading Mr Bloomfield to it, which was the 'job of work' he had specified,

THROUGH THE FENCE

but still . . . She began to feel rather mean about Janet. . . .

However, Mrs Bloomfield had begun to talk in her even, rather flat voice as they all drifted up the street together. She said it was a pity that Chris hadn't come with them that afternoon to a very, very interesting exhibition of historical relics. She said that even Janet had found it interesting; she had hardly been able to get her away from one of the cases. She said Mr Bloomfield and Willington had felt a little tired, and had gone right back to the hotel, but she herself was not in the least tired, and she proposed taking them all, now they had met in so lucky a way, to the nearest tea-shop to have an ice-cream.

Janet, who had been trailing along very quietly for her, now looked up. 'Could I have something else instead of ice-cream, please?' she asked.

'Why, yes, of course, dearie. Would you like cakes and a glass of milk instead? Or maybe they'd have strawberries and cream——'

'I didn't mean anything to eat,' Janet interrupted. 'I just wondered if plasticine cost the same as ice-cream. Because I would rather have a box of that.'

Pat looked shocked and angry. 'You've got a whole box of plasticine,' he pointed out, 'and it *isn't* the same as ice-cream. Ice-cream is what Mrs Bloomfield was offering you.'

'Yes, I know. But perhaps if I did without the ice-cream I could get a box of plasticine instead. I left mine in London.'

Mrs Bloomfield looked down at Janet. 'Now, you know, it isn't right for little girls to ask for presents. But

I really believe you meant to do without the ice-cream, so we'll just go into this store and see if they've got what you want.'

It was the toy shop where Chris had bought the ball. Mrs Bloomfield bought a large box of the plasticine for Janet, who thanked her and tucked it under her arm, ignoring her brother's scowl. Then they all went into a restaurant, and Mrs Bloomfield ordered ice-cream for four, which meant that Janet got some as well. Pat thoroughly disapproved of the whole thing, and began to talk to Chris, telling her about the exhibition they had been to.

As a matter of fact he had quite enjoyed it, although at first, when he had gone to meet Will at their usual rendezvous, he had been distinctly disappointed to find Mr and Mrs Bloomfield there too, and to hear that it was to be a cultural afternoon. However, they had the big car, although Pat was disappointed again when Mrs Bloomfield had insisted upon their driving all the way back to Caroline Square to pick up Janet and take her with them.

'What things were in the exhibition?' Chris tried to show interest, although she now felt suddenly tired and her feet as heavy as lead.

'Oh—old battleaxes, and a thing you executed people with, called the Maiden. There's a place to put your neck through, and then a knife drops and cuts it off. And a poisoned ring (I wonder if the poison's any good now?), and witches' charms, and so on. It was a medieval exhibition. It was pretty good.'

Mrs Bloomfield swallowed her last spoonful and called for the bill. 'I'm glad the rest enjoyed it,' she said, 'but I don't care for that sort of culture at all. It was Willington

THROUGH THE FENCE

who was wild to go, and I was real glad to find he took an interest in some sort of history. I'm sorry, though, that I took Janet. All that emphasis upon the different ways of killing people is very unfortunate.'

'But I liked it.' Janet looked up. 'I did, really.'

Mrs Bloomfield changed the subject abruptly, feeling that culture had taken an unfortunate turn that afternoon. Music was much safer. 'Do you know that the new Strauss symphony is being played the day after tomorrow? Pat has kindly said he can get tickets for us all through his father. Now, isn't that lucky?'

Chris tried to feel it was kind, but she didn't like symphonies. Pat looked a little uncomfortable. As Mrs Bloomfield got up and began collecting her things he said in a low voice to Chris, 'You needn't bother to go, you know. I don't think I will. But—well, Father said he could manage to get one or two, and it was a good way of returning the Bloomfields' hospitality.'

'I'm not going just to hear Mr Toscani play that solo bit,' Janet announced in loud clear tones. 'I'd sooner Mr Toscani dropped down dead.'

'Why, Janet!' Mrs Bloomfield became quite pink with distress.

'Yes, I would. Then Father's name would be up on those bills we saw on the way to the exhibition, and not Mr Toscani's. *Then* I'd go to the old concert, but not unless.'

'Father wouldn't dream of wasting a ticket on you,' Pat told her coldly; but Janet merely looked obstinate, and stumped along the rest of Princes Street averting her eyes from the posters which announced that the New English Orchestra were giving the first performance of

The Farewell Symphony by Richard Strauss, on Saturday night at 8 p.m. in the Usher Hall.

And before that, Mr Bloomfield would have his golden box! It wasn't any use trying to reach him tonight, because his wife said they were both going out to the theatre. But tomorrow morning, first thing, she would be round at his hotel asking to speak to him privately, even before the beds were made at home. . . .

Mrs Bloomfield had parted from them outside the restaurant. 'What's the matter with you, Chris?' Pat asked suddenly. 'You're crawling along like a snail. Can't you hurry a bit?'

'My feet are tired.' All the exhaustion of the afternoon swept down on her like a heavy weight.

'All right, let's take the tram.' But he looked at her curiously after they had boarded it, and when the tram turned off Princes Street he leaned forward and asked, 'Where have you been by yourself?'

'Oh, just exploring.' She would have liked to slump right back in the seat and close her eyes; but it was time to alight now, and she had to drag her feet along Caroline Square and up the steps. Janet shot past her with the new box of plasticine under her arm. Chris wondered vaguely why the child had been so keen upon getting it, but it seemed too much bother to think anything out to the end.

Nor could she eat much supper that night; she was too excited and tired. Even Mrs Bond noticed this with her bright boot-button eyes. 'You go up to bed and I'll help with the dishes,' she told her kindly at the end of the meal, and Chris was only too glad to obey.

Once in bed she felt better. The light still came in through the curtains, making a pleasant pink glow on the walls. She put her arms above her head and, half-asleep, began to plan dreamily what she would do tomorrow. She saw herself entering the big foyer of the North Caledonian Hotel, and asking to speak to Mr Bloomfield privately.

(' *Please tell him a lady wishes to have a private word with him.*')

Presently Mr Bloomfield would come down in the lift, all excited, with his eyes shining behind his glasses ; and she would step forward, saying, ' Mr Bloomfield, I've got good news for you. I've found the House of the Pelican. . . .'

He wouldn't even bother to wait to get out his car. He would start up the Mound with her, his long legs taking him so quickly that she would probably have to run to keep up with him. Now they had reached the Royal Mile. Now they were passing the high hoarding and going down the entry by the side of it. Now they were crossing a courtyard and going down another entry, and crossing another courtyard, and going down a little passage, and . . .

She started violently, quite awake now. The awful truth, which her excitement and tiredness had concealed till this moment, had burst on her suddenly. Again and again she tried to retrace her route by little pictures in her mind. Once more she saw, quite clearly, the entry she had gone through ; the creaking door and the little lane beyond it ; the grassy space and the fence and what lay behind. . . .

But she had forgotten how to get to the lane.

Between the first courtyard, where she had met Maisie Paterson, and the lane itself, there was only a confused remembrance of the way by which Maisie had led her. She had not even tried to remember it at the time. She could never find her way now, without help from somebody. Maisie would keep out of sight, since she had stolen her brooch. She would never find Maisie again, either.

Only one person could still help her now, and that was Effie. She must be made to, although she had seemed to deny any knowledge of the place where the old man was hidden.

Chapter XVII

EFFIE SAYS 'NO'

THE breakfast dishes had been washed and tidily put away. Chris followed her mother upstairs without a murmur, to help her to make the beds, because there was no hurry about seeing Mr Bloomfield now, and no use in it either. When they had reached Mrs MacKendrick's own bedroom, Janet tapped on the door and looked in.

'Have you got any pins?' she asked politely.

Mrs MacKendrick plumped up a pillow and then nodded towards her dressing-table. 'There are some in that wee box. Take what you want, but what do you need them for?'

Janet pretended not to hear the question. Chris saw that she helped herself to quite a number of pins, saying 'Thank you,' as she sidled rather quickly out of the room. She did not pay any attention, for she had her own problems to worry about, and Janet's odd desire for pins was not one of them. As soon as the work was finished she slipped downstairs, opened the front door and was walking rather quickly towards the tram stop in case her resolution might fail.

This was her last throw. She looked unseeingly out of the tram windows as the long stretch of Leith Walk unfolded itself. It was not a very elegant neighbourhood. Fish-and-chip shops, cinemas and cheap drapery stores flashed by almost unendingly. But now the docks and the blue waters of the Firth came into sight. She got out and smelt the fresh salty air, while the sea-gulls called shrilly above her head.

Where did Effie live? It was a thing the MacKendricks had never asked; but that did not bother Chris much, since all the fishing families knew one another, and she would only have to inquire. She walked towards the quays, and presently came in sight of a row of small houses with red-tiled roofs. Some of the houses had nets hung out in the air on stakes near their doors. A woman came towards her. Chris stopped her and asked, 'Can you tell me where Effie the fishwife lives?'

'Effie Elliot? Yonder, in the house at the end o' the row.'

Perhaps Effie would be away on her rounds. Chris hadn't thought of that till now. Perhaps it would have been safer to have come out to see her in the late afternoon. However, Chris was lucky that morning. No catch had been landed today, and Effie was doing some cleaning in the house. The door stood wide open, and she was on her knees scrubbing the steps.

'Well, now, so it's you!' Her round red face looked up pleasantly. 'Will ye no' step in? I've finished my steps and was just going to make a cup o' tea.'

Her little sitting-room was scrupulously clean. There was a three-piece suite in it, and a radio, for Effie made quite a lot of money with her fish. There were also two china dogs on the mantelshelf, staring into the room with round expressionless eyes. Chris would have been interested in them, were she not anxious about broaching the subject of her call.

Effie lit the gas-stove under a kettle, and while she waited for the water to boil she laid a clean cloth on a tray. Then she put two cups on the cloth and a plate of shortbread. After she had made the tea she poured it out and said briskly, 'It's real nice to have folks to share your eleven o'clock cup, so see and enjoy it, and the shortbread too. I made it mysel', wi' real butter.'

The shortbread began to choke Chris. Effie was being so jolly and kind she hated to have to tell her she had been following her like a spy, but it had to be done. She took a gulp of the strong hot tea and then said, 'I saw you yesterday.'

'Did ye now?' Effie did not seem in the least perturbed. 'And where was that?'

'Outside the House of the Pelican.'

The fishwife had been raising her cups to her lips. Her hand shook suddenly so that the tea slopped into the saucer. 'What's that ye say?' Her voice had changed too. It was loud, harsh and suspicious.

Chris leaned forward, speaking desperately. 'Listen, Effie! I wanted to find that old man who lives in it. I had a reason. A very good reason——'

'And what d'ye want wi' a poor harmless fellow like John Jamieson? Can ye no' leave him in peace?' For some reason she had grown suddenly angry. Chris was reminded of a hen's fluffing out and extending its wings to protect the chickens behind it.

'Who *is* John Jamieson? Why does he live hidden away there? What has he done?' A suspicion was dawning in the girl's mind. Perhaps the old man was a criminal. Perhaps he had even killed someone, and Effie was hiding him from the police. . . . She shivered suddenly, thinking of the little dark court and the old man lurking behind his shutters.

'Done?' the fishwife echoed indignantly. 'He's done nothing but refused to be put oot o' his ain house! Forty years he's lived in it and run his wee shop on the Royal Mile without ony interference from onybody. And now, just when he's retired and given up the shop, along come folks that tell him the old house is to be taken doon! Ay, everyone was cleared oot like cattle, though they were offered what they ca' alternative accommodation. But old John says there's nae alternative to the house he's lived in a' those years. So he finds a way back, and shuts himself up for fear they find him. If it wasna' for me and yon lass, Maisie Paterson, he'd be starved by now!'

'But they'll find him when they come to pull down the House of the Pelican!' Chris exclaimed.

'Ay, and I tell him that, but he'll no' budge. Mind you, I feel for the man. They'd no' get me oot o' *my* house either!' The fishwife took another gulp of tea to recover herself. But her suspicions recovered too. 'Ye'll no' tell onyone where he is? Ye'll no' give old Jamieson away?'

Now for it. Chris clenched her hands instinctively to give herself courage for the next words. 'I can't. I can't remember the way back to the lane. Maisie promised to take me to the house if I gave her my brooch. She led me by all sorts of twisty ways that I can't remember now——'

'*She* didna' give him away?' Astonishment and scorn echoed through Effie's voice. 'The wee limmer! I told him no' to trust her, but he said she'd hold her tongue for the half-croon a week he gives her!'

The reason for Maisie's actions now became clear. If the old man Jamieson were discovered and taken away, she would lose her weekly half-crown. So she had broken her promise to Chris and had run away before the end of the lane was reached, or the secret of the loose boards in the fence discovered. A great contempt for Maisie came over Chris. Effie kept the old man alive with her fish because she was sorry for him, though she thought him so foolish. Maisie just ran his errands and brought his food for what she could get. . . .

'She grabbed my brooch and ran away without showing me how to get there,' Chris told the other indignantly, 'and I can't remember how we reached the lane either. There are so many little courts and passages, I didn't think of noticing.'

A pleased look came over Effie's face. 'Weel, now, ye'll just be a good girl and forget ye ever saw the house, or John Jamieson either.'

'Effie, listen! There's a frightfully rich American here, and he wants something John Jamieson has. A wee gold musical box——'

'Ay.' Effie nodded her head. 'It was an antique shoppie he had, and nae doot he's got some o' his best stuff wi' him.'

'The American's willing to pay a lot of money for the box. He—he even promised two hundred pounds to the person who would find the house where it is. You can have half if you'll show us the way!'

To her astonishment Effie rose from the table, opened the door into the street and pointed towards it. 'Oot ye

EFFIE SAYS 'NO'

go, lassie! Wad ye try to bribe me to betray a friend o' mine?'

It had been a terrible mistake she had made, mentioning the money. She rose too, flustered, dropping crumbs of shortbread all over the floor. Beseechingly she turned to the fishwife. 'Never mind the money then! Couldn't you at least take a message to the old man? Couldn't he bring the box somewhere and show it to Mr Bloomfield? Then we need never go near his house at all.'

Effie shook her head. 'He'll no' budge from yon court in case some o' the neighbours see him and tell the police. Whiles, he takes a wee turn in it after dark, when he's finished his supper, but he'll no' go beyond, for he went as far as the lane once, and some wee boys saw him and thought he was a ghost——'

'One of them told me a witch lived there.'

'Ay. It's a good thing they're feared to go near yon court. But he'll no' step oot o' it, and I'll no' lead ye there. I've passed my word, and who's to say yon American 'll keep his mouth shut?'

Chris stood in the doorway now. She heard the dull clang of the shipyards and the scream of the seagulls flying overhead. Effie was edging her right out into the street. She opened her lips to make one more appeal, but the fishwife gave her a firm though kindly shove, and the next moment the door was closed in her face.

Chapter XVIII

PINS

'Have you got any spare pins, Mrs Bond?'

Janet had tapped on the door of the Bonds' room, and was now advancing into the middle of it. The time was just half an hour before lunch. Mrs Bond was preparing to go out immediately the meal was finished. She had laid her rather queerly shaped hat, with the large pearl pins, on the bed along with her bag and gloves, all ready to be snatched up at the last moment. Now she stood at the mirror, combing the grey fringe of hair which hung over her forehead.

'Pins, dearie? What do you want them for?'

'Oh, just something.' Janet sounded vague. She drifted over to the bed. 'Those are lovely big pins. I expect your hat would keep on all right with just one. Could you lend me the other?'

'Well to be sure! They're ornaments and not just to keep my hat on. Besides, what d'you want with a thing that size?'

PINS

Before Janet could answer there came the dull boom of the gong downstairs. Mr Bond appeared in the doorway. 'Come along, Mother. You'll have to cut pudding out again if we don't get started!'

Mrs Bond snatched up her bag, rather fussed. 'If it's ordinary pins you want, help yourself from the dressing-table. They're in the china tray. Coming, Father?'

Janet hung behind and followed them downstairs a few seconds later. Chris was letting herself into the hall as she reached the bottom step. The older girl looked tired and dispirited. She trailed into the dining-room and ate very little, her mother noticed. Presently the Bonds, as usual, pushed back their chairs, excused themselves and left the room. The telephone rang. Mrs MacKendrick sighed. She had been running about all morning, and did not want to bother to answer it. Besides, it would probably be a message for one of her guests.

As a rule Janet was not very free with offers of help. This time, however, she jumped up and said, 'Shall I answer it for you?'

'Yes, please, Janet. Away and see who it is.'

A heavy clump-clump announced the Bonds coming downstairs again. But the hall door did not close behind them as usual. Instead, they reappeared in the dining-room, and Mrs Bond's face, under the black-satin turban she called a hat, was flushed and angry.

'Where's Janet?' she asked.

'She's gone to answer the telephone,' somebody said. Mrs Bond half turned as if to make for the little telephone room, but her husband restrained her. 'Oh, come on, Mother! D'ye want to start the performance late on account of one miserable hat-pin?'

THE HOUSE OF THE PELICAN

They withdrew suddenly, like two of their own marionettes. The others sitting round the table heard them clatter down the steps after banging the hall door behind them. Pat, knowing his sister, looked uneasy. Mrs MacKendrick just looked surprised.

'What a queer-like thing for the Bonds to say!' she remarked, dishing out the rhubarb and rice pudding meanwhile. 'And what was all yon about a hat-pin?'

Janet seemed to be taking rather a long while to come back into the room. When she did she came in sideways, looking apprehensively about her. 'Have Mr and Mrs Bond gone out?' was the first thing she said.

'Yes, they have. Was the phone call for them?'

She slid into her chair again, looking relieved. 'May I have the rhubarb without the milk pudding? No, it wasn't. It was Mrs Bloomfield, and she gave me the message. She's got tickets for the Tattoo this evening, and she wants you and Chris and Pat and me to go with them. She says they'll call for us with the car at half past eight, and you needn't phone back unless you can't go.'

'Well, I'm sure that's very kind of her.' Mrs MacKendrick felt a thrill of pleasure and gratitude towards the Americans for so thoughtfully including her as well as her daughter. She looked across at Chris, expecting the girl to look pleased, but her daughter's expression scarcely lightened at all. One might have thought Chris hadn't even heard the invitation.

'That'll be a lovely treat, won't it, Chris?' She looked reproachfully towards her.

'What?' The other seemed to start out of some private and gloomy thoughts of her own. 'Oh, the Tattoo. Yes, Mother. It'll be fine.'

'Then you might look a little more pleased,' her mother said tartly.

Chris opened her lips, then closed them again. She couldn't explain, couldn't possibly explain that the Bloomfields' kindness only rubbed in her failure to find that box for Mr Bloomfield. She felt that she didn't even want to see Mr Bloomfield again. It would bring back her disappointment and failure too sharply.

Mr Foley was another person who was quieter than usual that day. Always a silent man, he was feeling pretty worn out by all the extra rehearsals made necessary by the performance of an entirely new and difficult work which the whole world was waiting to hear. He was too good an ensemble player to feel bitter about the choice of somebody else to play the effective solo part on his instrument; but the mention of Mr Bloomfield's name only emphasised what all the instrumental players in Edinburgh were aware of : that the disposal of several well-paid all-the-year-round posts in a first-rate American orchestra lay in his hands.

He was rather touched when Janet approached him after lunch with the suggestion that they should do something nice together. He had felt, sometimes, that his children did not see enough of him, and that Janet in particular was growing to look upon him as a stranger. 'What would you like to do?' He looked down at her, pleased.

'Couldn't we take a bus trip to some place far away ? Some place we wouldn't get back from for hours and hours.'

He nodded. 'But we'll have to get back in time for supper, you know.'

'Yes, I suppose so.' A sudden dejection came into her voice.

'Funny little thing!' he thought affectionately. 'One never knows quite what's at the back of her mind. . . .'

Chris felt greatly relieved when she saw the two of them sallying out together. She was really too tired, and too disappointed at her failure with Effie that morning, to have anyone tagging after her for the whole afternoon, wanting to be amused. She found a pile of illustrated magazines, and with them under her arm went into the empty drawing-room to get a little peace.

It was vast and still and soothing in here. She put her feet up on the sofa and stuffed all the cushions she could find behind her head. There was nothing to do until evening; and then she had the Tattoo to look forward to. . . . The whole house had grown empty and quiet. Everyone seemed to have gone out somewhere. The tiniest sounds were audible through the stillness: the tick-tock of the clock on the landing, even the gentle rustle and fall of the rose petals in the vase on the window table. . . .

Her eyes closed. It seemed only a moment before she opened them again and sat up, startled at the sudden decisive opening of the door. Mrs Bond stood in the doorway, looking in. Her face was red and angry, and her hat had slid out of the straight. 'Where's Janet?' she asked.

'Janet?' Chris rubbed her eyes. 'I think she went out somewhere with Mr Foley. Do you want her?'

'I want my hat-pin,' Mrs Bond replied, advancing a step or two and pulling one out of the back of her hat.

PINS

It was a long wicked-looking pin, with a huge pearl blob on the end. 'The neighbour to this,' she went on, holding it out, 'and a fine job I've had, trying to keep my hat on with only one.'

Chris stared, fascinated, at the dangerous-looking object. 'Did—did Janet take the other?'

'I'm morally sure she has. Morally sure. The girl has a perfect craze for pins—it's not healthy. Asking for pins all over the house! She saw these ones in my hat and asked for *them* too. When I went to put it on after lunch one of the pins was gone, and she'd been in my bedroom——'

'But what on earth could she want with one that size?'

'Goodness knows! But she's got it, I'm sure. And as I'm going out again to meet some friends of Mr Bond's I want that pin now.'

Chris scrambled off the sofa. 'They went off on some long excursion, I know——'

'So's Janet wouldn't be here when we came back! Oh, yes!' Mrs Bond snorted. 'But if you won't look in her bedroom, I will.'

They went to Janet's bedroom together. The child was wonderfully neat and tidy for her age, and there were no pins visible. Nothing in the little jewel drawers of her dressing-table; nothing hidden in the empty suitcase at the foot of her bed; nothing in the clothes drawers themselves. Not even one pin.

'That's funny!' Chris stood looking around her. 'You would think there would be some ordinary pins showing, at least.'

'What about the soiled-clothes basket?'

After all, they had looked everywhere else. Chris

took off the lid and rummaged. ' Oo ! ' she cried suddenly, stopping to put her finger into her mouth.

'What's the matter ? ' asked Mrs Bond, and Pat, who had just passed the open door, stopped, having heard the cry, and entered the room.

' Pins. One ran right into me.'

She lifted everything out of the basket and threw the lot on the floor. Then she peered in. ' What on earth— why, it's exactly like a hedgehog ! '

Right at the bottom of the basket there lay a little doll made out of pink plasticine. It bristled with pins stuck in all over it ; and Mrs Bond's big one, with the pearl knob at the end, was run right through the middle.

Pat shoved Chris aside and peered down at it in his turn. ' Gosh ! It's a bit like those witches' dolls in the show-case at the exhibition ! '

' Witches' dolls ? ' Chris couldn't imagine witches playing with dolls. She wondered what on earth Pat was talking about.

' Not real dolls, of course,' he was saying ; ' just little models in clay that they made of their enemies. Then they stuck pins or rusty nails into them and said some sort of spell that was meant to give the real people a pain in the same place. There were two old crumbly figures at that exhibition. . . . Yes, and Janet seemed absolutely fascinated by them. We could hardly get her away. . . .'

He and Chris looked at each other. ' I wonder who her enemy is ? ' Chris said slowly.

' Anyway,' Mrs Bond said, ' I want my hat-pin.' She leaned over, reached down and pulled out the long sharp thing. Then, having got what she wanted, she walked briskly out of the room.

PINS

There was a little silence. Pat looked uncomfortable and annoyed. 'I don't like it,' he said at last. 'I don't like a kid like Janet being able to hate anyone as much as that.'

He picked up a soiled towel lying on the carpet and bent over, as though he would lift out the little figure.

'What are you going to do with it?' Chris asked.

'Throw it in the ash-bucket,' he said briefly; 'and I'm going to give Janet a darned good row when she gets back too.'

The sharp ends of the pins were embedded in the little pink image, so it was not too prickly to lift. They went downstairs, Pat still carrying it in the towel, and Chris showed him the way through the kitchen, out at the back door, and where the big ash-bucket was, just at the area steps. Pat shook the towel out and the pink doll plopped into a pile of white ash removed from the kitchen stove that morning. Puffs of ash blew up in their faces. He jammed the lid on to the bucket again and turned back into the house, his face dark with anger and worry.

The long afternoon was drawing to an end. Mrs MacKendrick bustled in in time to make supper, and it was almost time for the meal before Mr Foley and Janet entered the house again. Mr Foley looked much more cheerful than usual. They had enjoyed the bus trip, which had been through the border country made famous by Sir Walter Scott's novels; and, in addition, Mr Foley had found an old friend on board the bus, a cornet player from another orchestra who was also taking the afternoon off.

Janet, as soon as she entered the house, became very quiet and subdued. One would think there was something on her mind. As soon as she came across Pat, she asked anxiously, 'Have Mr and Mrs Bond come back yet?'

Pat looked at her hard. 'Yes, they have. And Mrs Bond has taken her hat-pin back.'

Mr Foley had just placed his hat on the stand inside the door. Now he turned and surveyed his children. 'Hat-pin? What hat-pin?'

Pat explained, looking very coldly still at Janet. 'You remember those little witch-dolls, Father? The ones you saw when you went to the history exhibition by yourself? Janet went too, later, and has made one and stuck it all over with pins. Chris found it at the bottom of her clothes basket where she'd hidden it. I threw it away of course.'

Mr Foley looked quite bewildered. 'Well, why shouldn't she? Make one I mean. Did Mrs Bond lend her a hat-pin?'

'She *took* a hat-pin, and pretty nearly all the pins in the house as well. But it's not that. The silly little ass wanted to do someone harm. I'm quite sure she was trying the spell out. And—and she shouldn't feel like that about anybody, should she?'

His father made a sudden move and was just in time to grab Janet as she tried to slide past him upstairs. Mr Foley's expression had changed. He now looked severe and rather sad. 'Is that true?' he asked her. 'Were you really so wicked as to want to do somebody harm?'

Janet began to cry. 'I didn't want him to die,' she sniffed. 'I—I just wanted him to feel pins and needles so badly he couldn't play at the concert——'

'Wanted who? Tell me at once, who was the figure meant for?'

'Mr Toscani.' Janet was sobbing loudly now. 'If he didn't play at the concert, you would. And then perhaps Mr Bloomfield would invite you over to America, and give you a lovely little house where we could all stay together and not move around any more !'

Her father's hand dropped from her shoulder. Pat saw a very sad expression come over his face. After a minute he said, 'Listen, Janet. All that is nonsense and superstition, and you know it. But it's wicked nonsense. Wicked to wish anyone ill, and wrong to grudge anyone their success. Have I ever grudged Toscani his ? Did you ever hear me complain that some people got all the luck and others didn't ?'

Janet peeped timidly up at him. 'No, Father.'

'All your life you'll find some people ahead of you. Sometimes it's fair, and sometimes it isn't. All you can do is to play your own little part in the orchestra and save your breath for your job. To do anything else isn't just wrong, it's stupid.'

'Y-es.'

Janet's head now hung so low, he could hardly hear her ; but he patted her on the shoulder and said more kindly, 'Go upstairs and wash your face and hands. It's nearly supper-time.'

'She looks all out,' Pat said as they stood together in the empty hall and watched her disappear round the bend of the staircase.

'It was a long drive in any case, and I think she should go straight to bed after her meal. She seems to have forgotten about the Tattoo anyway. . . . You know, Pat, I *am* a failure, and I hate even Janet's recognising it. If I was a first trombone, with a permanent orchestra, we could all have a home together. She saw that all right.'

Pat felt very awkward and sorry for his father. 'You're a first-rate trombonist—everybody says so,' he told him warmly, ' and I think it's a great shame——'

Mr Foley stopped him with a gesture. 'That's the kind of thought I always have to struggle against. It's pure poison, and just makes things worse. One must look at the facts, and the facts are, that there are too many first-rate trombone players, and too few good solo parts for them to play. Why should I be luckier than anyone else?'

The supper gong boomed a few minutes later and everyone came downstairs except Janet. Pat went up to fetch her, and came down again to report that she was lying across her bed fast asleep. He hadn't liked to waken her, he told Mrs MacKendrick apologetically.

'Poor wee soul!' she exclaimed. 'I dare say she's just worn out with yon long drive. Chris, you take her some hot milk and biscuits and put her to bed properly.'

It seemed a pity about the Tattoo, but Janet was far too tired to go to it, and had evidently forgotten about it as well. Mr Foley muttered something about taking her to see it another night, as soon as the series of orchestral concerts was over. Chris heated a glass of milk and piled a plate with biscuits and bread-and-butter, and carried them upstairs on a tray.

Janet hadn't even bothered to take off her coat, but had flung herself right across the bed and was fast asleep. Her cheeks were still tear-stained, and her dark curly hair was rumpled and spread out against the pink quilt. Chris suddenly felt sorry for her, realising for the first time how much Janet wanted a home. She woke her quite gently, helped her to undress, and then put a large towel over her knees before she gave her the milk in case any of it should be spilt on the blankets.

Janet seemed only half awake as she sipped her milk. Presently, as Chris watched her, her eyes widened over the rim of the tumbler as though she remembered something. 'What did you do with Mr Toscani?' she asked in rather a shamed sort of voice.

'Mr Toscani? Oh, you mean the wee plasticine figure. Pat threw it away.'

'With the pins still in?' Her voice held a note of alarm.

'Yes, of course, except for the one Mrs Bond took. But it's all nonsense, Janet. Mr Toscani won't come to any harm.'

'Are you sure? I didn't want really to kill him. I only meant him to get pins and needles so that he couldn't hold his trombone properly——'

'He won't even get pins and needles, and you're too old now to believe in spells and fairy stories and rubbish like that. So finish your milk and then go to sleep again.'

Janet drained the last of the milk in a gulp, looking much happier. Chris took the tray from her rather impatiently, because it was almost time for the Bloomfields' car to arrive, and she wanted to make herself ready. When it did purr up to the door Janet had gone off to sleep so soundly she did not hear the little stir of excited departure throughout the house, or the front door closing.

And far beneath her, safe under the ash-bin lid, the little image called Mr Toscani slept soundly too, upon his mattress of dust.

Chapter XIX

JOHN JAMIESON'S FISH SUPPER

It was not quite dark yet, but that magic time when the sun has just sunk and left some colour behind it; when the sky is green, streaked with rose; when the lights shine softly like moonstones instead of hard and bright, and a few birds still fly through the air.

The lantern tower of St Giles showed scraps of pink through its open crown. The flowers had gone dark in the Gardens, though they would show themselves again presently when the concealed lighting was on, looking like a woman who has covered up her natural complexion with lots of make-up. The Mound was black with people crawling up it towards the Esplanade of the Castle where the Tattoo would take place. The Castle itself looked like something out of a fairy tale, with its towers and pinnacles melting indistinguishably into the massive outline of the rock, and the evening star beginning to show above it.

They had very good seats. Mrs MacKendrick, Pat, Will and Mrs Bloomfield were in the first row, and Mr Bloomfield and Chris sat behind them. The Bloomfields had brought out the rugs from their car because there was already a nip in the air, and it would grow colder as night came on. They had come very early too, because Mrs Bloomfield had a passion for earliness. At first Chris found it quite amusing to look at the big searchlights (not turned on yet) and the platform from which the commanding officer and other distinguished guests would watch the performance.

But presently she found herself talking to Mr Bloomfield to pass the time. She talked in a low voice because she did not want the others in front to hear what she was saying. Even while she was telling him all about her fruitless hunt for the House of the Pelican, she felt surprised at herself for doing so. Why should her adventures and her final disappointment come out now—and to him?

She might have understood the reason better if she had known that sitting quietly beside Mr Bloomfield had that effect upon many people besides herself. Most people found themselves telling Mr Bloomfield about their hopes and disappointments, if they were left alone with him long enough. He was such a quiet man, and he hardly seemed to be listening, which was very nice if one felt one might be sorry, some day, to have told him the things one had. This habit of sitting still and apparently not listening was quite a business asset to Mr Bloomfield. In that way many things came to be told him which he might not have otherwise known.

When she had finished he just looked down and gave her a kindly glance. 'You seem to have gone to a lot of trouble on my behalf. Thank you.' That was all he said.

'I did have an idea of following Effie next Thursday,' she went on rather hopelessly, 'because I heard her telling the old man she'd be round again then. But I can't hang around looking out for her all day. And now she knows I know about where she goes, she'll be looking out for *me*.'

'Why, yes, I suppose that's so,' Mr Bloomfield said, and lit a cigar.

An alarming thought took hold of Chris suddenly.

'You won't go and tell the authorities, so as to get them to let you into the house? You won't give the old man away?'

'Never dream of it,' Mr Bloomfield told her. 'I'd hate to do a mean thing like that.'

Somehow Chris knew that he wouldn't. She relaxed and began to watch what was happening again. The sky was much darker now. The last faint flush of colour had left it, and a few more stars pin-pricked the air above. They paled suddenly and disappeared as the big searchlights were switched on. A bugle sounded from somewhere, and then the trit-trot of horses' shoes. The searchlights swept round to pick out the raised portcullis and drawbridge of the Castle. Out from under the stone archway there swept a detachment of mounted

JOHN JAMIESON'S FISH SUPPER

Life Guards, their plumed helmets glittering, their uniforms blazing with scarlet.

Chris drew a sudden deep breath as the military band crashed into the air of a musical ride. Round and round swept the horses and riders, in and out, weaving an intricate pattern in the soft tan spread out on the enclosure. Down the middle paced Pompey, the fine old warhorse of the regiment, a drummer in the saddle, his kettledrums balanced on each side. The music pulsed through the night and the horses kept perfect time, galloping gently, sometimes in pairs as though they were waltzing together. Then, with a final triumphant sweep they all clattered over the drawbridge again, thundering past the two motionless stone figures of Bruce and Wallace, and disappeared behind the high walls of the Castle itself.

Even Mr Bloomfield was stirred. 'That was quite a spectacle,' he remarked to Chris, then stiffened again as a large body of Marines seemed suddenly to materialise on the great parade ground before them, drilling and exercising with clock-work precision. The Royal Air Force had its turn too, and then a scaling party with ladders showed how a fortress should be taken. But what thrilled Chris most was the acted scene in costume, showing the departure of Mary Queen of Scots for France as a little girl :

Two medieval trumpeters appeared on the ramparts above the portcullis. The lights picked them out in all their splendour of red and gold. She could see them put their trumpets to their lips, while the thin wavering notes seemed to blow away the present and bring back the past. Then a little cavalcade appeared slowly, moving under the portcullis, and trotted slowly across the vast empty space ringed by silent spectators.

It consisted of a small party of knights and nobles in sixteenth-century costume. They appeared to cluster about and guard the figure of a small girl mounted on a little pony. Her long blue robes entirely covered the saddle, on which she sat sideways. A rough-looking man in armour guided the pony by a leading-rein, and the little figure appeared to be swept onward, without any movement or wish of her own, towards her destiny and the scaffold awaiting her at the end. . . .

JOHN JAMISON'S FISH SUPPER

They vanished somewhere behind the ceremonial platform facing the Castle. The lights now played on the old building itself, that building which had seen so much of the little girl's history. Now one of the battlements was picked out where it seemed to hang over the steep rock and the invisible Gardens beneath. A mounted Lifeguardsman stood there motionless, silhouetted against the sky. He raised his trumpet to his lips and sounded 'Lights Out'. For only a moment he seemed to stand there, while the notes floated down to the city beneath. Then the searchlights switched off suddenly, dramatically. Horse and rider were blotted out in an instant, and the Tattoo was over.

The huge crowd began to make for the exits. 'Don't try to join us,' Mr Bloomfield called down to his wife and the others; 'in a scrum like this it's each man for himself. Make for the car, and if Chris and I don't turn up soon drive home. We can walk down on foot.'

It was as well that he said this, for while the front row of spectators were able to make for an exit quite easily by cutting across the great sawdust-sprinkled space in front of them, the rows behind had become jammed, and he and Chris had to wait a considerable time before they could take their turn at edging along down the gangway. By now, of course, there was no sign of any of their party. Mr Bloomfield's car had had to park pretty far down the Royal Mile, and the others had probably reached it and been forced to drive off by now.

'I guess the night air won't do us any harm though,' he remarked as they joined the crowd moving down it in a solid block; and Chris herself was quite pleased to prolong the adventure so as to keep in her mind, for a little while longer, the music and pictures they were leaving behind.

By the time they had drawn level with the Outlook Tower the crowd had begun to thin a little. Many people had turned off by Johnston Terrace, while others had taken the short cut down towards Princes Street which led by the side of Ramsay Gardens. A few empty spaces began to appear on the pavement before them. A cat ran straight across their path, and then, strangely, another and another. . . .

They were all going in the same direction, crossing the street and vanishing somewhere on the same side as that of the giant hoarding which now began to gleam white before them. One or two animals were slinking along the pavement itself. A large tom cat jumped down off a window-ledge as they passed it, and, plopping gently right at their feet, began to lope in a purposeful manner down the pavement before them, vanishing into the gloom beyond.

Mr Bloomfield paused to let a group of people just behind them pass on. 'See those cats?' he remarked conversationally. 'I'll bet they're all making for some place, and the same place too.'

'Why, yes.' Chris hadn't thought about the cats specially till that moment. Then a queer idea jumped into her head. 'You don't think——'

'Didn't you tell me those kids said all the cats in the neighbourhood visited Pelican Court after dark?'

'They said some nonsense about a witch and her cats. But of course there's no such thing.'

'Maybe not. But there's an old man who eats fish.

I guess he takes his supper about this time, and the cats know it.'

She felt herself shaken by a sudden excitement. 'So if we followed the cats we'd come to the House of the Pelican?'

'That's my idea. Let's try it anyway.'

They went on a few steps, then stood and watched, just beside the scaffolding itself. A cat slunk past right between their feet and vanished into the little entry beside it. Just to make sure it was not a stray one, they stood for a few moments longer. Three more cats went the same way, two from the direction of the Mound and one from the ledge over a shop front opposite.

'Here we go,' Mr Bloomfield remarked more briskly than usual, moving suddenly forward with a long loping stride, and following the last cat into the entry with remarkable speed. It was very dark, but beyond, a naked electric bulb shone high up in the ceiling of the covered passage, near the exit into the court where Chris had first met Maisie Paterson.

It was dark, too, in the court. A lamp, hung from a bracket fixed to the corner of one of the houses hemming it round, cast a faint light over the little paved square, throwing into deep shadow the mouths of the four narrow passages leading away from it. For a second or two the court seemed empty. Then two cats appeared, chasing each other out of the passage and streaking across to the one by the side of the light.

'After 'em,' Mr Bloomfield said simply, making for the passage down which they had disappeared.

But Chris hung back.

'It's no good after all,' she said hopelessly; 'we'll just

get lost, as I did, even if we do find the house first. We won't know the way back.'

'You've not got a piece of chalk in your pocket, I suppose?'

'Chalk? Oh, you mean so that we can make signs as we go along, as the tramps do. No, I haven't.'

Mr Bloomfield stepped right under the lamp and began to go through his own pockets. He brought out a book of stamps. 'A dollar's worth,' he said simply, 'but it's all in a good cause.' He detached a page of the stamps, licked it and slapped it on to the wall just under the lamp. 'Nicely labelled,' he remarked, stepping back to make sure the stamps showed properly, 'and we'll at least know if we get into the wrong court. I dare say they all have lamps.'

The passage too had its lamp, but it hung from the roof. All Mr Bloomfield could do was to gum another page of stamps on the wall, where the light struck them. He labelled the next court in the same way; and the next. If they were in doubt as to which turning to take, they had only to stand still a moment or two in the semi-dark, and then followed the next slinking shape where it led.

A lamp hung in the hooded archway with the iron door at the side of its twisting stair. The door was closed, and the cats must have found some scaleable wall that would lead them into the lane beyond. Chris had a sudden fear that the door might be locked. But it wasn't, and they pushed it open, to see the lane she remembered lying before them.

'Don't waste any stamps on that door,' she said quickly; 'the lane doesn't lead anywhere else but where we're going.'

Mr Bloomfield put his stamp-case away, and they began

JOHN JAMIESON'S FISH SUPPER

to walk down it. No lights shone down from the windows of the deserted houses on either side, and it was very dark. Chris was glad that Mr Bloomfield was with her, because she would never have dared to go down the lane alone. The abandoned washing-green at the end of it looked pale grey in the light of the moon which now had a little space to show itself in.

'Look!' She pointed suddenly towards a cat that had just sprung down from the fence and was slinking by. It held in its mouth what looked very like the tail of a large fish....

'Supper's being served,' Mr Bloomfield remarked, as they went towards the fence. Chris felt for the loose boards and he helped her to prise them out as gently as possible, so as not to make a noise. Then they both knelt down on the grass and peered through the open space.

Pelican Court was yellow with light. The shutters, behind which John Jamieson lived, were flung open, and a big oil lamp on the window-sill lit up a circle of light in the darkness beneath it. Cats of all shapes and sizes were moving restlessly about the yard, sometimes growling and spitting at one another, sometimes emitting a yell of hunger. The only quiet ones were those who had been given their pieces of fish already. They had retired into corners with them, or were making off already for the fence and the privacy beyond.

Silhouetted in the window was old John Jamieson himself. He was scraping a frying-pan vigorously so that the scraps and pieces of skin fell down, to be pounced on by the cats below him. 'Now then, ye rascals!' he called down to them, 'nae fighting! Awa' and clean up the court instead o' makin' yon noise!'

THE HOUSE OF THE PELICAN

Mr Bloomfield began to wriggle through the fence. Chris followed him cautiously, and he jerked her free on the other side, pinning her where she stood. 'Keep out of the light!' he whispered, 'Work your way round to the foot of the steps. . . .'

The circle of lamp-light left a fringe of darkness under the high walls which hemmed in the court. They felt their way round the walls, and presently found themselves at the foot of the little wooden staircase leading to the jutting-out addition to the old house. Here they were hidden from the old man leaning out of the window, thanks to the deep shadow it cast. The door at the top of the staircase was standing ajar. They could see a yellow streak of light coming through it.

The American darted, panther-like, for the steps. Chris followed him, stepping as softly as she could. They were through the door in a flash before the old man had time to do more than turn, startled, from the window, with the frying pan in his hand.

'Pardon our intrusion,' Mr Bloomfield said very politely, 'but have you a small gold musical box for sale?'

Chapter XX

MR BLOOMFIELD MAKES A DEAL

The old man looked both astonished and frightened. 'Who are ye? Where did ye come from?' he exclaimed.

'My name's Bloomfield, and I'm a visitor to Edinburgh. I collect rare old musical boxes. I have reason to believe that you possess one—you showed it to a little girl the other day, didn't you? If I like it, and you are willing to sell, I would give you a very good price.'

Chris had cast a quick glance round the room while the others were talking. There was a dingy wall-paper, peeling off at the corners to reveal the thick stone of the walls. A piece of stone carving surmounted the fireplace, in which a rusty stove burned. A shelved recess on one side contained some old china ornaments, a few long-stemmed glasses and the old man's hat. On the other side was an ancient door, bolted and studded with iron nails.

John Jamieson had had time to get over his fright and become suspicious. 'Are ye goin' to tell the police I'm here?' he asked sharply.

'The police? No, why should I? That is, if you aren't harbouring stolen goods.'

'Stolen goods?' He bristled. 'Everything in this room's mine. Bought and paid for. When I gave up the antique dealer's business I brought my favourite stuff here, just for my own pleasure, ye understand. I've done no crime that I know of, unless it's a crime to refuse being put out o' one's own house!'

THE HOUSE OF THE PELICAN

'I see. Well, we won't give you away. But I'd sure like to see that box.'

The old man shuffled over to the recess beside which Chris was standing. He hesitated, then half boastfully, half lovingly, began to display his treasures. 'This plate's real Meissen—I sold the rest o' the set to a London dealer when I was clearing the shop, but I kept one back for a souvenir. Yon's a wee snuff-box that was aye a favourite o' mine. See the bonny enamel lid?'

It was easier for Mr Bloomfield to conceal his impatience than Chris, for he was at least interested in the old fellow's treasures. But he drew a sharp breath of relief and anticipation, when groping, John Jamieson brought out at last the little gold box. Its owner walked back to the lamp and held it under the light. There it was, almost the twin of the one lent by Lord Drumfingal. He touched the spring, and into the close dark little room there rolled a burst of pure nightingale song. . . .

Mr Bloomfield took it reverently between his own hands. He felt the gold box throbbing as if it had a heart inside it instead of machinery. The bird threw its little gold head back and forward as it sang. And Chris, who had never heard a nightingale in her life, suddenly remembered a green wood in spring, a wood near the village they went to for holidays, and almost saw the little stream that echoed and caught the voices of the birds in the wood.

The machinery clicked, and the box ceased to throb. The bird stood motionless now on its lid. Mr Bloomfield laid it gently down on the table beneath the lamp. 'To think one can buy and sell a miracle like that!' he said. 'All the same, I do want to buy it, so name your price.'

'It's all very well,' John Jamieson answered, 'but what good's money to me?'

'Well, you've got to live, haven't you? Live and eat. I dare say you've got to pay for the fish you buy.'

A cunning look spread over the other's features. 'Ay, but I've money enough in a wee hidey-hole in the wall! Don't ask me to show it to you because I won't. And as nobody kens I'm here, I don't have to pay rent. See?'

Mr Bloomfield began to walk up and down the floor. He had to persuade the old man, somehow, to take his money. 'Look,' he said abruptly, 'you can't possibly *like* living on here. For one thing, the workmen may finish their job on the Royal Mile any day, and arrive to take down the house. What will you do then?'

'Go and board wi' a friend o' mine called Effie Elliot,' the old man said obstinately; adding 'no' that I'd like being in someone else's house, me that's aye had my own. But though I've enough saved and hid away to live on, I've no' got enough to buy a place o' my own. And if they want to put me in a rented one, they'll have to drag me feet first. Thae nice modern bungalows! I fair hate them with a' their conveniences and hot-water taps!'

Chris suddenly saw what he meant. The bright little bungalows with their cheerful flower-gardens and electric gadgets were a very different matter from, for example, Effie's own house which was certainly old and no doubt lacked a bathroom, but was cosy and familiar to anyone who belonged to the past.

'If you could buy a little house like Effie's, all to yourself . . .' she began tentatively.

Mr Bloomfield was on to the suggestion like a flash. 'Why now, that's an idea! You'd get an old-fashioned cottage far cheaper, surely, or maybe even be able to rent one. And I'll write you out a cheque for five hundred English pounds here and now, if you'll give me the box!'

John Jamieson thought for a moment. 'It's true,' he said slowly. 'Effie warned me the men were coming any day now to gut out the inside o' the old house; and I'd like to buy my own place. But what use is your cheque to me? I've no' used a bank, let alone crossed the floor o' one, since I got orders to quit and hid mysel' here.'

'All right. I'll bring you the money in pound notes if you like. Tomorrow.'

There was a struggle going on in the other's mind. At last he nodded reluctantly. 'I was thinkin' maybe it was time to clear out in any case. Well, I'll accept your offer. But mind, ye don't get the box till ye lay the money out on yon table!'

'Sure, sure. I'll get it just as soon as the banks open tomorrow, and I'll be back!'

Chris was staring around the room. In spite of its dinginess, some attempt had been made to keep the place tidy. The bed in the corner was spread with a fairly clean cover, and the old man's clothes hung from hooks on the wall. But she was looking for something else. John Jamieson's eyes were on her, and he guessed shrewdly at her thoughts.

'Don't you be looking for my hidey-hole, for ye'll no' find it,' he warned.

'I was just thinking how nice and tidy you keep things here,' she told him hastily.

'Well, maybe. But it's the yard that's given me a headache. Ye ken, the refuse men dinna come there now, and I've to burn everything in yon stove. I save the heads and tails o' Effie's fish though, and throw them out to the cats when I've had my supper. They'd make a gey stink in the stove.'

He saw her glance towards the old iron-studded door and grinned. 'It's not behind there either! Yon's just the entrance to the main part o' the house. This room was built on to it, above the yard to serve—what d'ye think it served? As a prison. And a prison for a leddy too!'

She remembered the old story suddenly. 'Lady Drumfingal!'

'Aye, the poor creature. I never rightly knew what she'd done, but anyway her husband built on this room and kept her here till she died. Many a time I've thought o' her and me both prisoners in the same room, wi' maybe two hundred years between us. But I could walk out when I liked, and she couldna'.'

Mr Bloomfield glanced towards the other newer door by which they had come. 'I suppose that was made long afterwards?'

'Aye. And the steps leadin' down to the yard. When the Drumfingals left the big house naebody of note would take it—they were a' for living in the New Town. So the rooms were let out as lodgings, and the new entry and wee wooden staircase built up to this one to give a separate way in. Yon old door's been nailed up for long enough. Ye couldn't open it now if ye wanted to.'

Chris glanced towards it again. It looked ominous and secret. She imagined the deserted half-ruined old house behind it; silent and mice-ridden, it was due to be opened to sun and air any day now, as soon as the men with the pick-axes arrived. . . .

Mr Bloomfield was moving towards the other door

now. He cast a fond glance at the musical-box as he passed by, obviously wishing he had the right to put it into his pocket. John Jamieson held the door open for them, but as they began to go down the steps he uttered a warning.

'Ye found me out, I dinna ken how. But mind this: one word to anyone but yourselves, and ye'll never get the box. I'll smash it to smithereens myself!'

'We'll not say anything,' Mr Bloomfield called back hastily, 'and we'll come back tomorrow—alone.'

'Mind ye do what ye say. If I catch sight o' an official with ye, I'll smash yon box afore ye've time to get up the steps!'

They heard the door bang behind them and a bolt being drawn into place. The shutters were slammed too, before they had left the court. The House of the Pelican seemed to disappear behind them into the dark, and the hole in the fence beyond seemed just a black mouth, through which they entered, to cross the dim patch of grass and enter the lane behind it.

The old door under the archway stood open the way they had left it. They walked round the court, searching by the dim light of the lamp-post in the middle for the pasted-up stamps. Taking the narrow passage nearest to the pale label glimmering on the wall, they arrived at the yard beyond, and by the same means, following the clues Mr Bloomfield had left, came out at last on the Royal Mile.

It was past midnight now, and the whole city lay quiet. The trams had stopped, so no sound came up from Princes Street far below. A few lights still glimmered in windows here and there, but the illuminations in the Gardens had been turned off, and Sir Walter Scott's monument was

MR BLOOMFIELD MAKES A DEAL

only a dark silhouette against the stars. They walked down the Mound, and Mr Bloomfield picked up a cruising taxi at the foot of it. He ordered the taxi to drive to Caroline Square, so that he could see Chris safely back home before driving to the hotel himself.

There was a light still burning over the hall door of the guest house. Scarcely had the taxi stopped when Mrs MacKendrick herself flung open the door. 'Is that you, Chris? Where on earth have you been, lassie!'

She was relieved when she saw Mr Bloomfield getting out of the cab too. 'My apologies,' he said politely, 'but Chris and I had a walk through the Old Town, and I guess I didn't keep proper tab of the time. It was very interesting. But we ought to have remembered your natural anxiety.'

'Well, I wasn't so very anxious, seeing she was with you,' Mrs MacKendrick told him frankly, 'and then Will said how they couldn't wait for you with the car, which had to be driven out of the way of the crowd. But I hope she'll be able to rouse herself tomorrow morning, that's all.'

Chris looked quickly at Mr Bloomfield. Her mother had turned back towards the hall. The American took the opportunity of saying in a low voice, 'I'll draw the money first thing, and be back at the hotel before half past ten. Meet me there if you want to see the box handed over.'

She nodded and then ran into the house.

Chapter XXI

JOHN JAMIESON SEEKS A NEW HOME

THE foyer of the hotel was comparatively empty. She saw him standing beside the reception desk when she dashed in, breathless, having managed to escape from the house without telling her mother she was going out or where she was bound for. She felt rather mean about this, especially when she remembered the huge pile of plates waiting to be washed beside the sink; but what else could she have done if she were to keep her promise not to give away old John Jamieson's secret?

'Come on,' Mr Bloomfield was saying abruptly; 'we're going by car. I've a hunch that the sooner we reach there the better.'

They parked the car at the top of the hill, and went once more down the entry by the side of the boarded-up houses. Not much hammering came to them as they passed the hoarding, and the suspended platforms seemed empty of men clambering about them. The courtyards were empty of children too, for Scottish schools begin their autumn term early in September, and everyone was at school.

The school Chris went to opened again the following week. It was lucky that she was still on holiday and able to see this adventure through to the end. The stamp-labels were easy to find by daylight, and she saw now the point of Mr Bloomfield's sticking them so high up the walls. Had they been within the reach of Maisie Paterson and her friends they might have been all scraped off already.

They entered the little lane beyond the old doorway, and began to go down it. On both occasions when Chris had traversed it before she had been struck by the surrounding silence and loneliness of the place. Now some echoes from the outside world seemed to reach it; echoes of dull blows and crashes, and the far-away sound of men's voices shouting. . . .

'How queer!' She stood still in the middle of the lane. 'I didn't think you could hear the workmen from as far off as this!'

Mr Bloomfield seemed to have a premonition of what was happening. 'Come on, hurry!' he cried, and began to run with long loping strides down the lane.

The noise of falling stones grew louder and louder as they approached the washing-green at the end. Mr Bloomfield clawed at the loose boards in the fence and pushed his way through, not even turning to give Chris a hand. When she had wriggled through after him an amazing scene met her eyes.

The little wooden staircase leading to John Jamieson's abode was dotted with his treasures: small groups of porcelain figures stood beside old silver candlesticks, and a bundle of clothes was flung down carelessly on the bottom step. The old man darted out as they approached, carrying another precious object out of the house. After laying it down he shook his fist at the high bit of boarding which cut off Pelican Court from the houses nearer the Royal Mile.

'Ye limmers!' he shouted. 'Wad ye start tearin' a man's house down about his ears?'

Then Chris caught sight of the object threatening the little house at the top of the steps. The men had not yet taken the hoarding down, though they were hammering at it already, invisible but clearly audible; and above the hoarding itself was thrust the upper half of an iron tripod, whose great chain carrying the heavy ball on its end had already begun to sway. . . .

The sheer-legs! She had seen how it worked; she knew that the next minute the iron ball would come through the air and go smash through the rickety upper half of the house. 'Keep away!' she screamed. 'Don't go back up the steps!'

The old man stopped, startled by the sudden sound of her voice. The old Chinese vase he was carrying slipped through his hands and lay shattered on the hard stones of the court. None of them had time to notice that however. For the iron ball on the end of the chain had suddenly appeared through the air, landing square on one of the shuttered windows, crashing clear through the rotten wood with a tinkle of broken glass.

The ball swung back, disappeared, and then began its

slow arc again. The old man watched, petrified, until Mr Bloomfield shook him by the arm.

'The house is finished!' he said. 'Get away before the men begin to come into the court!'

'No' without my things!' John Jamieson answered between his teeth.

The iron ball still struck well above the little staircase. He dived for the steps, with Mr Bloomfield after him. Together they clawed up the precious objects he had saved from his old stock and brought them farther off to a place of safety.

Mr Bloomfield made the trip again and again. He seemed to be searching for something. Then he looked up and measured the retreating ball with his eye. A second or two would elapse before it returned on its arc, to widen the gap in the side of the house.

'You forgot the musical box!' he shouted over his shoulder. 'I'm going in to get it——'

He had already taken three steps up the staircase when Jamieson's voice halted him. 'Come back, Yankee fool that ye are! I've got the wee box in my pocket!'

He pulled it out triumphantly and held it aloft; but the jerk had released the mechanism, and through the rattle of the chain on the sheer-legs and the falling of stones and glass, the little bird's song began to pour forth. It sounded as though rejoicing at the fall of the house. John Jamieson said, 'T'ts!' in an annoyed tone of voice, pressed the spring and reduced it to silence.

Mr Bloomfield came slowly down the steps again. He was rather pale. 'Maybe that was a crazy thing to do,' he said rather shamefacedly as he joined them. Stooping down he began to pick up as many of the things lying on the ground as possible. 'You take those candlesticks, Chris. I'll put the snuff boxes in my pocket and carry this bowl. I dare say Mr Jamieson can manage the rest, but the sooner we're out of this place the better.'

Laden with what they were carrying they went back the way they had come. When the people on the Royal Mile saw them emerge they stared a bit at the curious procession, and then, probably deciding that the tall man and the girl were just helping some antique dealer to change his stock, hurried on after one glance. Mr Bloomfield led the way back to where his car was parked. He opened the door and gestured John Jamieson in to the back seat.

'Have you any idea where you want to go?' he asked.

John Jamieson huddled himself in one corner of the car, his best possessions on the seat beside him. Now that the excitement and danger were over, he looked suddenly very collapsed and old. 'Drive me to Effie Elliot,' he muttered at last; 'Effie the fishwife, ye ken. She's a kind woman. She'll take me in.'

'I'll show you the way,' Chris told Mr Bloomfield quickly, climbing in beside him.

So they drove all the way down to Leith. As they passed by the quays, Chris caught sight of Effie filling her creel from a fresh-landed catch of herring dumped on the harbour edge. She pointed her out to Mr Bloomfield, who promptly steered his car as near as he could get to the edge of the quay. Effie looked up and saw them. When she saw John Jamieson too, her mouth opened in astonishment and she came hurriedly towards the car.

The old man leaned out of it and spoke to her. 'Well Effie, it's happened. They're bashing my house to pieces. Can ye take me in?'

'Surely I can!' The kind woman made a gesture towards where her house stood, and then addressed the American. 'If ye'll run him back there, I'll follow ye directly. I was goin' on my rounds this mornin', but that'll just have to wait.'

They halted patiently before the neat little house with its red roof until Effie came up. She drew a large key out of her pocket, inserted it in the lock and threw open the door. 'Just you bring in his bits and pieces, I'll mak' ye all a cup of tea,' she said over her shoulder.

There was a scrubbed kitchen table in the middle of the room, and on this table they carefully placed all that was left of the old man's possessions. Effie did not heed them much; she was too busy filling the kettle and laying out cups and saucers. John Jamieson surveyed the remnants of his worldly goods rather sadly. Then he wrenched the little gold box from his pocket and held it out to the American.

'If ye have the money wi' ye, it's yours. I left some two-three pounds back in the hidey-hole yonder, but they'll be destroyed or taken by now. There was no' much left anyway, and I'll need to pay Effie for my keep.'

Mr Bloomfield took out his notecase and counted the money out. He had drawn it in five pound notes and they made a huge pile on the table by the time Effie turned round and stared at it, wide-eyed. The old man had watched the counting narrowly. Then he nodded his head, satisfied.

'Yon's my last deal,' he said as he handed the musical box over, 'and it's no' a bad one, I will say that. The wee box was nothing but trouble and care to me. I was aye feared it wad break down, and me no' able to mend it. But if ye've the money to buy it, ye've the money to keep it in order.'

'Losh!' Effie breathed. 'Ye'd think my house was a bank!'

Mr Jamieson's eyes had begun to wander thoughtfully round her kitchen, looking for another hidey-hole. Mr Bloomfield, guessing what was in his mind, said to him. 'You don't need to be afraid of going into banks now, you know. You aren't hiding from anyone any more. I'd put that money in a bank at once, if I were you.'

Effie looked at him gratefully. 'You're right there, sir. I wouldn't sleep a wink wi' it in the house!'

It was arranged that she would take her new lodger to bank his money that morning, and also to buy some night-things and a shirt or two, for the little clothing he had had was now lost among the ruins of the room that had been

JOHN JAMIESON SEEKS A NEW HOME

Lady Drumfingal's prison. 'And I can buy something for our dinner as well when we're passing the shops,' she said.

The old man shuddered slightly as a thought struck him. 'Not fish, if ye don't mind, Effie,' he begged; '*not* fish!'

Mr Bloomfield and Chris said goodbye and went back to the car. The American sat still in the driving-seat for a minute or two before starting. He wanted to gloat over his box. He pulled it out of his pocket and took it gently between his hands, stroking the little gold bird. 'I'd like to compare it with Lord Drumfingal's,' he said at last, putting it back with a sigh of satisfaction. 'I'll bet the same craftsman made both.'

Chris didn't say anything. Her mind was full of new mattresses. She wondered if he had forgotten his promise. He hadn't.

'And I owe you five hundred dollars,' he added, 'for a job well done. Would you like if we went to the bank now and drew it in five pound notes?'

Chapter XXII

IT'S AN ILL WIND...

MRS MACKENDRICK could hardly believe her eyes when her daughter, charging into her room, slapped down the packet of notes she had brought from the bank. They were neatly held together in a rubber band, and she had carried them home in a big blue envelope, holding the envelope tightly with both hands all the way in the car.

'Chris! Where on earth? . . .' She stared down, bewildered, as Chris snapped off the band and began to spread the notes out on a table to make them look as many as possible. She listened to the story of the gold box. She gasped when she learned how nearly her daughter (along with Mr Bloomfield, who didn't matter so much) had been in the part of the House of the Pelican which was destroyed just before they could enter it. And as soon as the tale was ended, because she was so relieved, she began to scold.

'You had no right to wander about like that, especially after dark. No right at all!'

'But I didn't go there alone after dark! I was with Mr Bloomfield. The times before, it was quite light. Janet was the one who shouldn't have gone. But if she hadn't, we'd never have known that the box was in the House of the Pelican, and I'd never—Mother, do you realise there's a whole two hundred pounds in this room? Now we can get some new mattresses, and maybe put up our prices next season!'

IT'S AN ILL WIND...

Triumphant though she was, Chris felt something was due to Janet. She decided that when they went out to order the mattresses, she would keep back some money to buy Janet something really good. Even a piece of jewellery perhaps. Janet loved jewellery and was always borrowing bits of it to wear for a while. Or, maybe, a small watch on a strap....

She waited to pounce upon Pat when he came in for lunch. At first the boy would hardly believe her, and when he did, he was more than envious. Not about the money, she was glad to notice, but about the adventure he had not shared. He decided to ring Will Bloomfield up as soon as the meal was finished, to suggest their going along to see the House of the Pelican for themselves.

'I think you can get right in from the Royal Mile now,' Chris informed him, 'because they'll have taken down the boarded-up bit at the side of those old houses, so as to get to it more directly. I'd love to come with you, but Mother and I are going out shopping.'

When Pat got on to Will at the hotel the American boy sounded enthusiastic about meeting him and doing a little exploring. He told Pat, however, that he couldn't have the car. His father had taken it to drive out to see Lord Drumfingal and show him the box.

Chris waylaid Pat again before he could leave the house. She told him about wanting to buy Janet a present, and asked, should it be a necklace or a watch? Pat hesitated, but looked pleased for his sister's sake.

'I should say a watch. She'll need one anyway in a year or two's time, and it would save Father having to buy one then. Necklaces she can jolly well do without.'

So after the MacKendricks had visited the big furnishing

shop and had chosen their mattresses, they went to a jeweller's and bought a very pretty little watch for Janet. Then they came home, and encountered Pat just coming along the Square. Mrs MacKendrick was in a hurry to get back indoors so she went on, but Chris walked more slowly to hear what Pat had to say.

He and Will had managed to reach the House of the Pelican without any difficulty, since the blocked-up passage leading directly to it had now been cleared. Strictly speaking, they should not have been allowed on the scene of operations at all; but a kindly foreman had let them through, and they had found the old courtyard cluttered with all the implements for demolition.

The wooden staircase had been cleared away already. The little room at the top of it, which jutted out and spoiled the symmetry of the old house, was being demolished, stone by stone. The foreman remarked that somebody must have been living in it, because an iron bedstead and some old clothes had been found. Also the stove blocking up the old fireplace had been still warm when they hauled it out.

'Some tinker body, maybe,' he had said; adding, 'though how the inspectors managed to miss him beats me.'

The boys had vouchsafed nothing to this remark. They hadn't wanted to give old John Jamieson away. They asked if the whole of the old house was going to be taken down, and the foreman had said no. It was now scheduled as an ancient monument, and as soon as the rotting floor-boards were renewed, the walls repaired and any dangerously decayed cornices supplied with new stone, it would be opened to the public as a museum.

They should not have been allowed on the scene

IT'S AN ILL WIND . . .

'Queen's Pleasance, it's called,' the foreman had said, 'but I mind when it had another name, though it's mostly forgotten now, and I canna remember it myself.'

Will had glanced thoughtfully at the sculptured stone pelican above the entry on the courtyard side. 'Something to do with pelicans?' he had suggested.

'Well now, ye've hit it!' the foreman exclaimed. 'The House o' the Pelican . . . I remember it fine. It belonged to a great family once, and the talk was, that the pelican was their crest. Ay, and there was some sort o' tragedy or murder or somethin' connected wi' the house that gave the family a scunner at it. Anyway, they left long ago.'

Chris was deeply interested by Pat's recital. She wondered if Mr Bloomfield would like to go and see the old house too, but Pat thought not. 'Didn't you know they are leaving Edinburgh tomorrow? They're only staying over tonight because Mr Bloomfield wants to hear that Strauss symphony. He's mad keen on hearing it, not only on account of the music, but'—here Pat sighed—'because the Fairport Orchestra cabled to him that they need a first-rate trombone player for their next season. He's pretty sure Toscani will do, but naturally he wants to hear him first.'

Chris gave Pat a sympathetic glance. 'If only your father——' she ventured.

'Oh, well, Father'll get his chance some day, I suppose. I dare say he's lucky always to find a job when he wants one, though it does mean moving about from one town to another. Still, it's awfully bad for Janet. Not having a home, I mean.'

With all the excitement of finding John Jamieson and

the musical box Chris had forgotten that the big concert was tonight. Mr Foley would no doubt want his supper early, as he always did when the New English Orchestra was playing. She went into the house quickly and through to the kitchen to remind her mother.

Mrs MacKendrick was rolling out pastry in quite a leisurely way. The meat to go inside it was in a stew-pan on the gas stove, and not nearly cooked. Chris lifted the top of the pan, sniffed at the meat and then said, ' Oh, well, he'll have to do with an egg. I can boil one and put it on a tray in five minutes.'

'Who'll do with an egg?' Her mother paused to flour the rolling-pin, speaking quite absently. She was planning in her mind which bedrooms were to have the new mattresses.

'Mr Foley, of course. Didn't he remind you the orchestra was playing tonight? He usually does.'

'Oh, him?' Mrs MacKendrick looked relieved. 'He's had something to eat and gone off already. I told him to help himself any time he was in a hurry, so Mrs Bond says he's had a glass of milk and some biscuits, just to carry him through the rehearsal——'

'An extra rehearsal? Why?'

'Mrs Bond says he got a phone message when we were out. It seems some player that was doing a solo has gone down ill, and he's to take the part at short notice——'

Chris nearly dropped the egg she had been absent-mindedly holding. 'Do you mean Mr Toscani, the trombone player? Is he ill?'

'Ay, that was the name. I knew it reminded me of an ice-cream shop. Mrs Bond says as soon as he got the message he was off like a shot. She says she had to fairly

IT'S AN ILL WIND...

force a glass of milk down his throat, and stuff his pockets with biscuits—why, what's the matter, Chris? Where are you off to?'

'To tell Pat,' gasped Chris as she bolted out of the kitchen.

She rushed up to the drawing-room where he generally hung around until meals were put in. He was standing at the window looking down on the Square. 'Pat! Mr Toscani's ill! And your father's got the solo part to play after all——'

'*What!*' Pat swung round in amazement.

'Mrs Bond knows about it—she was in the house when they phoned. Oh, Pat! I do hope Mr Bloomfield likes the way he plays!'

Pat's eyes shone; but he kept a steady grip on himself. 'Don't suppose one ought to be pleased at another fellow's ill luck,' he muttered; adding, 'I wonder if Toscani's illness is serious?'

'What's the matter with Mr Toscani?' A sharp little voice sounded from the doorway. Janet had come in and stood there, looking frightened.

'I don't know. But they've phoned Father that he's ill, anyway, and can't play tonight——'

'Oh! I made him ill, but I didn't mean it! Do you think he'll die? It's your fault, Pat, you should have taken the pins out . . . I *knew* they shouldn't be left in!'

She was trembling now, and very white. For a second or two they couldn't think what she meant. Then Pat remembered the little doll stuck over with pins. 'Don't be ridiculous, Janet!' he told her sharply. 'The pins have got absolutely nothing to do with it. You don't even know what's the matter with him; he may have been sickening for something for weeks.'

'Couldn't you find out? Couldn't you please find out?'

'How can I? Don't be silly. Father's the only one here who might know, and he's gone to rehearsal. Besides, they mightn't have told him over the phone.'

Janet's face looked so pinched and anxious that Chris said hurriedly, 'Mrs Bond was in when the phone message came, wasn't she? Perhaps he told her.'

Janet turned and shot out of the room. They heard her begin to climb the last flight of stairs leading to the floor where the Bonds' room was. They generally used it as a sitting-room during the day.

'Come on,' Pat said; 'we may as well hear any news there is. . . .'

Janet had knocked and gone into the room by the time they appeared behind her. Mr and Mrs Bond were sitting very cosily, one on each side of the unlit fire, playing Patience on the little card table before them. Although not usually startled, they seemed quite surprised at the agitated way in which Janet made her request for information.

'Why, yes, your father told me about poor Mr Toscani while he was sipping his milk. Appendicitis it is. A nasty thing too. Seems he had had some attacks before, but had put off the operation till after the Festival——'

'How long before?' Janet asked breathlessly.

'Well, now.' Mrs Bond placed one card carefully on top of another before she replied. 'Where was it he had that last big attack, Father? You know I told you how Mr Foley said he really thought his chance had come that time, but the pain went off and so Mr Toscani played after all.'

'Chester,' said Mr Bond, laying a red ten on a black knave. 'It's coming out,' he said, alluding to the game.

'Chester? Why, that was in spring!' Pat exclaimed with an illogical feeling of relief. He turned to his sister. 'There you are, you little ass! He's been suffering from it for months!'

Janet looked greatly relieved too, but still a little uneasy. 'Where would he have the pain exactly?'

Mr Bond was a man of few words. He did not make any reply other than that of indicating a spot on his waistcoat, slightly to the side.

'Oh, there? That's not where I drove the big pin in. I stuck it in right in the middle.'

Pat looked at his watch and began to fuss. 'I rather want to hear the old man play that bit myself. He gave me those complimentary tickets, so if anyone wants to go to the concert too——'

The Bonds shook their heads like mandarins. Mrs Bond said, 'Many thanks, but Father isn't a bit musical. Doesn't know one note from another. And I've got his socks to darn. Though I'm sure we both wish him the best.'

'Certainly,' Mr Bond said. 'Much obliged,' he added, waiting patiently for them to take themselves off and leave him free to concentrate on his game.

So there were two more tickets to spare. Mrs Mac-Kendrick, like Mr Bond, wasn't really musical, but she liked a big concert in the Usher Hall, with the thrill of a large audience and the fun of going out somewhere in the evening without paying for it. Chris was just beginning to enjoy the symphony concerts she sometimes heard over the radio. Janet and Pat wouldn't have missed hearing their father play solo for the world.

Mrs MacKendrick had a cold supper hastily assembled together. Janet put on the new watch which Chris gave her, and Chris wore her best dress and made herself as tidy as possible, thinking of the audience and the occasion. They all felt happy and excited as they went out into the cool of the evening, although they had to stand in the tram, which was packed with other concert-goers all bound for the same place.

Chapter XXIII

THE FAREWELL SYMPHONY

THE huge dome of the Usher Hall stood up blackly against the evening sky. The flower-beds before the main entrance had been planted with stocks which gave off their fragrance now that the sun had sunk. Car after car slid round the curve of the great building, setting down smartly dressed people, and being moved on by policemen, who also marshalled the queues in order.

Pat led his little party proudly past the people who stood by the kerb in a long line, patiently hoping for the chance of returned tickets or a seat in the gallery. This concert was one of the high-lights of the Festival, and all reserved seats for it had been sold months before. Inside, the foyer was packed with people and the corridors thronged. Pat's seats were downstairs, at the back of the hall. He felt a little apologetic about leading his guests to places so far away from the platform, but Mrs MacKendrick assured him kindly that she did not like being too near the brasses—they always seemed to be blowing her away.

The members of the orchestra were on the platform already. One could hear their tuning up, over the buzz and movement of a vast audience seating itself. The harpist was clawing at her big gold harp in an experimental fashion, and one of the violins was playing a little scrap of melody over and over again.

Mr Foley sat at the back, with his trombone over his

THE HOUSE OF THE PELICAN

knee. He wasn't practising anything, but staring right before him. Janet stood up and waved, but Pat pulled her sharply down into her seat. 'Don't *ever* signal to a player,' he warned, 'or you may put him right off. Anyway, it isn't done.'

'Oh!' Janet clapped her hand over her mouth, appalled. Supposing her wave had managed to put her father right off his few bars of solo? Still, he looked so very far away, a mere blurr on the platform, she comforted herself by deciding that he couldn't possibly have seen her anyway.

A man in a white tie and tails came out from the back of the platform with his violin under his arm. There was some polite clapping, and Mrs MacKendrick thought it was the conductor and that he was perhaps going to play the violin as well. However, Pat told her it was only the first violinist, and that he generally got a cheer. Suddenly all the players stood up. A short tubby little man walked briskly forward, stepped on to the rostrum and bowed right and left. The cheering became much louder, for he was a world-famous German conductor who had flown over specially for this concert alone. The orchestra crashed into *God Save the Queen*. Everyone stood up. And then the concert began.

It began with the Beethoven *Leonora* Overture, and Chris was delighted to find that she seemed to know it already, as it had come over the radio once or twice when she happened to turn it on when she was dusting. That made it much easier to listen to, and she found that she really liked it. Both Pat and Janet had been trained, if they listened to music at all, to listen to it intently, so one really couldn't tell whether they were enjoying it or not.

THE FAREWELL SYMPHONY

Mrs MacKendrick, who wasn't really musical, only liked it in bits. Half-way through her attention wandered. She began to run her eye round the grand circle, where the important people sat; the people who had come in evening dress and could afford all that money for their seats. She stiffened, grabbed Chris by the arm and whispered, ' Look, there are the Bloomfields ! '

' H'sh ! ' Chris warned, shaking herself free; but she glanced up too, and there indeed they were, right in the front row, Mr Bloomfield wearing a white tie like the men in the orchestra, and Mrs Bloomfield with her hair immaculately waved and with a mink cape over her shoulders. Willington sat between them, but she couldn't see his expression.

The overture finished, and the cheering broke out again. ' Do you see the Bloomfields, Pat ? ' Chris leaned across Janet and indicated them.

' Yes,' Pat answered briefly. It was an almost unendurable strain to watch Mr Bloomfield sitting aloft up there, with his lean poker-face and his glasses on. He had an unopened score lying on the plush hand rail before him. Pat knew that it must be the score of the Strauss Symphony which came on after the interval. He felt somehow that when the moment came to open that score he wouldn't be able to look at Mr Bloomfield any more; that he wouldn't be able to look at his father either, in case the trombone should come in at the wrong moment, or Mr Foley be suddenly smitten with some disease like Toscani, and didn't come back to the platform at all. . . .

He was relieved and thankful when the interval came. The others wanted to leave their seats and walk about for a bit, and he felt too restless to remain where he was, so

THE HOUSE OF THE PELICAN

joined the crowd leaving the hall, presently finding himself at the foot of the great staircase with its silken hand-rope and curved marble sides.

'I would like fine to go upstairs and see all the dressed-up folk,' Mrs MacKendrick was saying wistfully at his elbow. She had only a blue afternoon dress on herself, but decided to forget about it as such an opportunity was not to be missed.

'Yes, let's go up,' Janet exclaimed, 'and then perhaps we'll meet the Bloomfields.'

The long curving gallery upstairs was banked with flowers. A big recess, at least the size of Mrs MacKendrick's drawing-room, held a sofa and chairs, and groups of smartly dressed people lingered here, talking and look as though they were posed for photos in the glossy magazines. All the time there was the swish-swish of hundreds of people walking back and forth over the marble floor. Snatches of conversation in all sorts of foreign languages reached them; Spaniards, Americans, Indians, Africans all went by as they watched, as though being brought slowly before them on a conveyer belt.

The Bloomfields came by at last. Janet darted forward eagerly to detain them. 'Did you see Father playing at the back?' she demanded. 'In the next piece he's going to play all by himself!'

Mr Bloomfield nodded. 'I know. I want specially to hear him. Enjoying the concert?'

Janet brushed his question aside. 'If you like the way he plays, will you——'

'Shut up!' Pat said fiercely, trying to elbow his little sister away.

Mr Bloomfield gave him a kindly sympathetic glance.

THE FAREWELL SYMPHONY

He seemed to have guessed just what Janet wanted to say, and to know the breathless hopes of both brother and sister. 'Whether I like it or not, I've a little proposal to make. This is our last night in Edinburgh, so what about collecting your father after the concert and all of us going to have supper somewhere?'

'Why, Ambrose!' Mrs Bloomfield demurred. 'Don't you think it would be a little late for such young people? Not for Mr Foley, of course. I guess it would be a privilege to entertain a musician entrusted with so important a part in this great new work. But Janet——'

'Janet's going right home with me,' Mrs MacKendrick said firmly; adding, 'it's very kind of you, I'm sure, but I have to get up early, and wee girls should get their sleep. Of course if Pat——'

'Can't I go too, Mother? I'm just as old as Pat!' Chris looked pleadingly at her mother, who relented. 'Very well then. But mind, no coming in after midnight, like yon night after the Tattoo!'

Mr Bloomfield hastily said that he would guarantee to drive the Foleys and Chris right back home after supper. Then the bell sounded to warn people to go back to their seats. The marble gallery began to empty, and as they passed by the flowery recess they saw that everyone had left there too. They had only just time to regain their seats before the conductor walked on, raised his baton, and the first bars of the Strauss *Farewell Symphony* crashed through the hall.

So far as Mrs MacKendrick was concerned, it seemed to go on and on. Sheer noise, she said to herself, glancing with surprise at the absorbed faces of the music-lovers sitting around her. Even Janet was restless, fidgeting now and then under Pat's stern glance. Far away and high up, Mr Bloomfield opened the score before him, bending over it intently. But Pat kept his eyes on his father all the time; and when the intricate jumble of sound died down suddenly, he was waiting for the lonely note of the trombone, playing by itself with electric effect after the tumult preceding it.

'Very pretty, I'm sure,' Mrs MacKendrick presently leaned forward and whispered kindly. Somebody 's'shushed' her from the row in front, and she felt quite affronted. Wasn't it only polite to say something nice to the boy and girl belonging to the man who had blown those notes all by himself, to a big listening audience like that?

She felt very like saying sharply, 'That's Mr Foley, and he's staying in my house,' but the moment had passed. The symphony was nearly over. The rest of it was lost upon Janet who, now that the strain of waiting for her father to come in was over, had fallen asleep. But Chris was quite sorry when the last note came. She had just begun to make something of the music, and it was a something far bigger and more wonderful than was ever contained in the light sweet music the hotel orchestras sometimes played over the radio.

She came back with a bump to the present. Waves of cheering had broken out all over the hall. The conductor came back again and again. Now, this last time he had paused before coming forward. What was he doing? He was taking Mr Foley by the hand. He was leading him right up to the edge of the platform. He was shaking hands with him before all the people. And Mr Foley, his long face looking whiter than ever, was making a bow, first to the conductor, and then to the cheering audience itself. . . .

Janet sprang to her feet and cheered too. Nobody stopped her this time. Pat was clapping as hard as he could, and Chris, looking at him, saw there were tears in his eyes. It was a moment of triumph for them all. They could scarcely speak when at last the cheers stopped and they left their seats to join the queue making its way up the gangway towards the nearest exit.

Mr Bloomfield had told them where he had left his car, and that they were to wait beside it until he could collect Mr Foley. Mrs MacKendrick led Janet firmly towards a tram; but Chris and Pat worked their way through the crowds spilling out into the wide space before the hall. Drinking in the calm night air with relief after their excitement, they made for the little side-street where the Bentley was waiting.

They stood there, not speaking for a while. Then Chris said rather shyly, 'What do you think Mr Bloomfield's saying to your father, Pat?'

'Don't know,' Pat answered shortly. 'One thing I *do* know though, and that is, that Toscani couldn't have played any better.'

Mrs Bloomfield and the two men approached in the light of the street lamps. They seemed to be talking as they went along. Pat noticed that his father looked rather dazed, but he often did just after the strain of a concert. Mr Bloomfield was whistling softly. He seemed very pleased about something.

'Well, my lad,' he exclaimed more heartily than usual, 'how do you think you'll like life in the States?'

'Do you mean? . . .' Pat glanced at his father, scarcely daring to breathe.

'I'm sending a cable off to the orchestra back home. I think I've found them their new trombone player.'

Mr Foley still said nothing at all. He climbed into the car beside his host with his trombone case neatly beside him. The car regained Princes Street and they drove past the Gardens bordering it, with the flower-beds, all lit up, lying between the glimmering statues and about the foot of the great Scott Monument, with Sir Walter sitting, high and aloof under his stone canopy. From end to end it was a fairy scene, and the vista was closed by the Calton Hill with its high Greek pillars bathed in light.

Mr Bloomfield had booked a table at his hotel, and ordered a very special supper. Chris wondered once or twice what her mother would say to her eating hot lobster at that hour of night. She noticed that Mr Foley only pecked at his, but that was because he was so dazed with thinking about the future. One can be turned to a stone statue oneself through excitement, if one happens to be made that way.

The only words that she caught passing between the two men, was after they got up to go. 'I'm sending the cable first thing tomorrow,' the American said, 'and though I can't guarantee an engagement, I think they'll take my say-so.'

Chapter XXIV

A LETTER FROM AMERICA

The return cable arrived a day or two later, after the Bloomfields had left Edinburgh for a little tour in the Highlands. It offered Mr Foley the post of first trombone player in the Fairport Orchestra, at a salary which almost stunned him. The management of the Fairport Orchestra followed this up with a letter, asking if he would be prepared to sail for America in a fortnight, with his passage paid and also the passages of his family. It was a permanent post, the letter explained, and rehearsals were due to start almost immediately, as the winter season would open in

October with a performance of the new Strauss symphony.

Mr Foley was a changed man after receiving that letter. The look of care went from his face and he even made little jokes. He also paid several visits to Mr Toscani in hospital, taking him expensive flowers and grapes, and was greatly relieved when Mr Toscani told him that he had an old mother living in London, and wouldn't have gone abroad and left her for anything.

The Festival drew towards its close. Only a few days of it were left, and just one more performance of the Bond Puppet Theatre which had been very successful and made quite a lot of money for Mr and Mrs Bond. They seemed to spend most of their time making long arithmetical calculations and adding up rows of figures. Once, when Pat had gone to a travel bureau to confirm their passages, he saw the Bonds leaning confidentially over the counter of the American Travel Section.

It was Janet who found out what they were planning. One evening they appeared to be so busy up in their room, that they could not have heard the supper gong. Janet offered to go and tell them the meal was in. She found them seated, as usual, before their little card-table, but Mr Bond was very busy with some bits of wood and a pot of glue, while Mrs Bond sat watching.

He had made a miniature tea-chest. It was roped with cord and fastened with miniature red seals. On each of the square sides he had painted H.M.S. *Tea* in large black letters. Mrs Bond was arguing with him. They paid no attention to Janet.

'It reads like the name of a ship,' she was saying rather crossly.

A LETTER FROM AMERICA

'Well, maybe it does,' Mr Bond conceded, 'but Boston won't think so. Boston 'll take it at once.'

Mrs Bond snorted. 'Bet you the Boston people have forgotten what His Majesty's Service meant long ago.'

'It 'll remind 'em,' her husband said grimly, beginning to blacken the letters with the small brush he had picked up.

Janet approached the table. 'What are you making that for?' she asked.

They glanced towards one another. Mrs Bond nodded. Mr Bond said, 'Well, we'll let you into the secret. What d'ye think of our taking the Bond Puppet Theatre over to America?'

'Other folks can go to America besides the Foley family,' Mrs Bond said. 'But I must say it was your father's success that put it into our heads. That and the Americans over here who came to our show and liked it.'

Janet's quick mind leaped to the possible meaning of the little model box. 'Are you doing a new play over there? Has it got something to do with tea?'

Mrs Bond told her the story of the tea that was thrown into Boston harbour in the days of King George III. She explained how the American colonies had wanted to be independent, and thought they should not be taxed from England; how tea had carried a high tax and, when a shipload arrived at Boston, the people were so angry at being asked to pay the tax they had thrown the tea into the harbour.

'I'm makin' a model ship, and an artist fellow I know can fake the harbour for me with looking glass,' Mr Bond interrupted proudly. 'Blue glass,' he added; 'it 'll set off the redcoat uniforms best.'

'Father thought of dressing a puppet like King George III, and making him walk about, shouting and waving,' Mrs Bond went on, 'but I told him that was plain silly. King George never was in Boston in his life.'

'All the more reason to let the Boston people see what he looked like,' Mr Bond said stoutly. Catching his wife's eye he weakened. 'All right, Mother, all right. Historical accuracy, that's the ticket. Anyway we're going over in the same boat with you people—we've just heard this morning that they can book us a passage. We're opening in Boston, and then going on to Fairport. So mind you come and see us there!'

After that Janet spent the next day or two watching the Bonds making red uniforms for the British soldiers who would come on to the harbour to guard the tea, and quaint costumes for the Colonials who were to throng the little stage and help throw the tea into the harbour. Mr Bond whistled as he worked. He whistled *Yankee Doodle* and *Marching through Georgia*, and tunes like that, trying them over to see which ones would make the best background music. 'I'll get records of 'em,' he remarked; adding hopefully, 'or maybe the audience 'll do the singing. We'll see.'

The Foleys had to go off to London to collect their things and be ready to sail from Southampton, and the Bonds left soon after as well. The Festival came to its climax with fireworks let off from the Castle ramparts, and the big cannon booming at midnight. After that a great stillness seemed to fall upon Edinburgh. Princes Street looked almost empty after the crowds. The flowers received their first touch of frost, and began to look slightly pinched. People all told each other how tired they were after so much culture and all the friends they had had to entertain ; and Mrs MacKendrick rang up the painters to ask them to come and redecorate the hall.

She felt she could afford this, because she intended to charge just a little more from now on, on account of the comfortable new mattresses. Chris started school again. Each day when she came home for dinner she found an awful smell of paint inside the house, and painter's ladders and pails lying about everywhere. It was exciting to see the hall changing colour a little more each day ; but the regular boarders went about with their handkerchiefs over their noses.

One day she turned briskly into Caroline Square and found herself wondering how old John Jamieson was getting along. Effie had told them he had sold the rest of his treasures, getting such a good price for them that he was able to buy a fisherman's cottage which happened to be empty, and settle down nicely. She began to wonder what the cottage looked like, and if the old man would care about seeing her again. It was a half-holiday, and she had almost a mind . . .

The leaves were falling from the trees in the Square and blowing across the road. Soon it would be winter. Mr Foley, in a white tie and tails, would be playing with his new orchestra. The Bonds would be travelling through America, stolid and square as they always were, and she hoped they were being a success. She sighed. It would have been nice to have gone to America too. Then she remembered what her mother had said ; that, if the winter was a success they might even take one of those ten-day trips to Switzerland after Christmas, when things were quiet. . . .

THE HOUSE OF THE PELICAN

She opened the hall door and was met by the usual smell of paint. At once she saw the American air-mail letter lying on the table. It was addressed to her, so she pounced on it and tore it open. Some snapshots fell out. One showed a very pretty house with a big porch and a lawn in front of it. Mr Foley was cutting the lawn in his shirt sleeves. Janet sat on the porch step looking all rigged up and rather affected. Pat must have taken the photograph, because he wasn't in it at all.

But he had written the letter.

I hope you like our new house. We have a frig. and central heating and all the trimmings. Everyone has, here. I'm getting to like school, though I didn't at first, things were so different. Will Bloomfield is in my class, he's a fine sort of chap and put me wise to a lot of things. Father's playing in Boston next week. I guess the Bonds haven't turned up yet, but we certainly mean to see their show when they do. Will says to give their respects to the old fellow who had the musical box, and his father hopes he doesn't miss it. He's perfectly crazy about it himself.

Chris read the letter over twice. It made Pat sound rather strange and different already. As if he had turned into an American. 'Put me wise.' 'I guess.' 'He's perfectly crazy about it. . . .' But they would stay the same inside, she was quite certain of that. Especially Janet. Nothing would stop Janet's play acting or becoming excited, though maybe as she grew older she wouldn't tell stories so much.

Somebody was heavily stumping down the area steps outside. She heard the fishwife's call at the back door. 'Caller-oo! Caller-oo!' It was the day Effie always

A LETTER FROM AMERICA

came. She ran through the hall, down the steps leading to the area, and opened the door at the end of the kitchen passage.

Effie had her basket on the steps already. 'I've some fine fresh haddies here. Bring you a plate, lassie. Or wad ye like me to gut them at the sink?'

Chris nodded and led the way back to the kitchen. Effie whipped out her sharp knife and her scrubbed board and began to clean the fish in the expert way Chris admired so much. A vision of all the cats who had once streaked towards John Jamieson's window came over her. 'They'll miss Mr Jamieson's fish suppers down in Pelican Court,' she said.

'Aye, the pussies 'll mourn him. But wad ye believe it, old John 'll no' look at a fish nowadays! Ye ken, it was a' he had to eat, except for a pie or a sausage or such that Maisie Paterson brought him. He was feared to go to the shops in case folks knew him and asked where he was living noo. It was maybe only me and my fish that kept him alive. And now he's right off them.'

Chris thought privately that this was very understandable; but she only asked if he had settled down nicely in his new home.

'He likes it fine,' Effie said, 'but he's a wee thing lonely, whiles. Could ye no' go and see him? He's got a real nice wee house. Just two doors from mine, it is. There's the name, Dolphin Cottage, painted over the door.'

Chris memorised that, and decided she would go and see him that very afternoon. She would take the snaps from America too. Maybe he'd be interested. When Mrs MacKendrick heard about her plan she said it was lucky she'd baked that morning, because the old man would probably like some scones and also a home-made cake. She wrapped the freshly baked things in grease-proof paper, and Chris set out.

It was windy and cold down by the Firth. A big ship kept hooting in a melancholy manner, and all the fishing-nets had been taken in because there was not enough sun now to dry them. Chris came to the row of old-fashioned cottages which still stood from former days, a memento of the old fishing life of the place. One of the cottages had recently been repainted. Its paint was very bright blue, and the name DOLPHIN COTTAGE was painted in large white letters over the door.

She lifted the knocker of polished brass and let it bang heavily twice. The door opened, and there stood old John Jamieson, not looking in the least surprised to see her. 'So it's you!' he said. 'Come away ben.'

The cottage had only two rooms, a kitchen and a little bedroom opening off it. Everything was scrupulously neat and tidy, and Chris suspected that Effie was keeping it so. A cheerful fire burned in the quaint old fireplace, because John Jamieson had strenuously opposed any more modern type of heating. What immediately caught her eye, however, was the one ornament in the room. It was a staring china dog, and it occupied pride of place right in the middle of the mantelshelf.

'Effie gave me yon,' the old man told her, seeing her look at it; 'it's one o' the pair she had. She saw I was wearyin' for my china and glass that I had to sell, so she gave it to me. She's a good soul, Effie.'

Chris handed him the parcel of cakes and scones. He

untied it, fetched a big blue-and-white plate, and examined each specimen of her mother's baking before he laid it down, weighing the scones in his hand.

'Fine and light,' he remarked, 'and the cake's properly fired too. Give your mother my compliments and my best thanks.'

She then showed him the snapshots that had come from America. He studied the one of Janet carefully. 'A bonny wee thing, I mind her distinctly,' he said, handing it back; 'awful taken up with my musical box she was. I wouldn't have asked her in, but she looked too wee to remember where she had found me.'

'They've got a lovely house, haven't they?'

He shook his head firmly. 'It's no' my idea of a house. Yon flat roof, and a' these windows. No privacy. Not even a hedge. . . .'

He went over to the mantelshelf, lifted the china dog, and took from underneath it a small newspaper cutting. 'There's a house for ye!' he said, handing it over. Chris looked at the bit of newspaper. It showed a photograph of the work being done behind the Royal Mile. There stood the old house of the Drumfingals, scaffolded up to the roof, but with the courtyard cleared of its out-buildings and rickety staircase, and with the stone bird above its entry newly cleaned and pointed up.

'I see how Janet made her mistake,' she said slowly. 'She told us you lived in a house with a stone bird carved above the entry to the court. Either she'd got muddled and forgot, or we didn't ask but just thought that the pelican would be on the side of the entry facing the street. So of course we hunted up and down the Royal Mile, but we never found it.'

THE HOUSE OF THE PELICAN

'Ay.' He took the cutting back and slipped it under the white china dog again. 'Old Lord Drumfingal 'll be real pleased to see his house looking respectable again. And I hear, now they've found out whose it was, they're goin' to give it back the old name. Queen's Pleasance, indeed! The folks around never called it that, anyway. No. It's to be called the House of the Pelican, the same as it always was.'

Walter ✓
Gilbert ✓
Douglas ✓
Marion ✓
Morgan ✓
Jean ✓
Joan ✓
Carol ✓